She continued to approach him. "I am obligated to inform you that your contract is currently being interpreted under the Indentured Forces Act." The gun was now touching the man's chest. As he looked down at it, his face changed and he raised his hands. Griffin felt a wash of relief. Michaels knew she meant it.

"Failure to cure this breach," she said, and raised her gun to his neck, "could result in substantial penalties." She pushed the gun's muzzle into the soft underside of Michaels' chin.

For a long still moment, Griffin was afraid she might blow Michaels' head off right in front of them. Please, no. Please don't do it. Griffin was afraid to breath. Michaels blinked. Cranshaw did not. She waited.

Quantum Gate®

A Novel

Jane E. Hawkins

PRIMA PUBLISHING

Foreword

Stories are funny things. Like lovers they possess you. Some go away, some you stay with for the rest of your life.

Quantum Gate, seems to fall into this latter category. It has consumed the past four years of my life and now, as evidenced by the book you hold, it refuses to depart. Fortunately, given the current incarnation, this is a good thing. Good because Jane has done a superlative job of bringing the story of *Quantum Gate* into the world of paper and ink and good because I am allowed to see it fresh.

Quantum Gate actually began life during the Gulf War. One night while watching a murky CNN broadcast of an Iraqi missile attack, it occurred to me how easily the event could have been faked. Indeed, they could have told us that a nuclear weapon had been used against Baghdad and, if supported with the appropriate movie magic, we would have believed it. How would we have known otherwise? This seed, after a bit of embroidery and speculation, took root in the year 2057.

The first incarnation appeared, under the title *No

One Dreams Here, in HyperBole, the on-line interactive entertainment magazine which I published for several years. Built in Macromind Director for the Macintosh, at that point it would seem to have little in common with the live-action, high-production interactive movie it would shortly become.

Next came a company called Media Vision (a huge misnomer, as we would eventually discover) and the chance to fully develop *No One Dreams Here* for CD-ROM using 3D sets (as opposed to the hand-drawn backdrops of the earlier version) and live actors (as opposed to clip art and scanned images). We said yes. There were however a few caveats: they needed the whole thing in six months (a ridiculous schedule—as anyone in the world of software development can attest) and we had to move to Seattle from Houston (a great opportunity—as any Seattle resident can testify). Oh, and we had to change the name. *No One Dreams Here* was too long. *Quantum Gate*, the marketing folks decided, had a stronger appeal to all those teen-aged boys who were destined to become our customers.

In order to accommodate the "ship it for Christmas or die" schedule which faced us, we were forced to cut the story in half and greatly reduce the number (and depth) of the interactive elements. This bothered us considerably more than it bothered the publisher. Towards the end of our six months in the

Media Vision gulag, we all realized that daily trips to our homes and contact with our families were seriously interfering with our productivity, so we set up tents and sleeping bags inside our development studio. I am not making this up. We'd work until too exhausted to go on, then crawl to a pile of bedding, sleep for a few hours and get up and keep going. Eventually, perseverance, hard work, and endless compromises all paid off, and *Quantum Gate* was ready to be permanently etched into all those shiny discs. It won many awards, was lauded by some, and lambasted by others. As one of the first interactive movies for the personal computer, it was born with something of an identity problem. We never set out to make a computer game. Personally, I don't enjoy computer games. We intended to create a story which the player can participate in and experience in a new way. In that, we succeeded. We didn't do quite so well at setting people's expectations properly. Media Vision's marketing machine made *Quantum Gate* sound like a frenetic, sci-fi, blast-fest. It was, by design, anything but that.

Once *Quantum Gate* shipped, we almost immediately began work on *The Vortex*, the "second half" of *No One Dreams Here*. I could tell you about Media Vision's compulsory script changes ("more sex and guns"), their bankruptcy (turns out they were all a bunch of crooks), or our mad scramble to stay afloat after they walked out on the hundreds of thousands of dollars they owed us to finish the project.

It would sound all too commonplace to anyone really familiar with the world of entertainment or media.

Suffice it to say that we survived and managed (somehow) to complete *The Vortex* for a 3 disc CD-ROM and publish it ourselves. It too won many awards and kudos. It too was lambasted by people who couldn't conceive of anything other than a game. All of which simply brings me up to the present and why it is that Jane's version of *Quantum Gate* is so precious to me.

In many ways it represents the real story. It is *No One Dreams Here*, before years of compromise and short-sightedness. Before being bullied, conned, and threatened by unscrupulous hucksters looking to cash in on our work.

It is a joy to be able to return to those ideas and characters which first presented themselves to me, four years ago. It is a joy to find them rendered here with such heart and skill. It is a joy, which most of all, I am happy that we can share.

—Greg Roach

Chapter One

Something was critically wrong, and Private Andrew Griffin had no idea what it was.

Beside him, the other members of his platoon stood at attention, each waiting to take the solitary walk into the heart of the Quantum Gate, and into whatever unknown waited on the other side. Griffin surreptitiously wiped his palms along the seams of his trousers as Private Michaels swaggered into the center of the huge chamber. Castle had already vanished into the flashing lights and hollow roar; now Michaels stood at attention, looking impudent and hip, and light gleamed from his shaven skull. Griffin stared at him, and Michaels winked back. Cocky bastard—perhaps he hadn't heard—a beam of pure red light shot up around him. Twelve bronze crystals rose like the immense petals of a closing flower, hiding Michaels from sight, and the roar reached a crescendo. Griffin winced and it came again, the same way it had with Castle—over the roar, over the rush, a thin, high noise, almost beyond hearing—a thin, high noise like a man's scream.

Something was desperately wrong.

Then all the noise disappeared and Griffin stared into a moment of pure and shocking silence, before the great gold crystals petaled open to reveal an empty center. Griffin's shoulders tensed. If he could, he would have turned and ran—but the crack troops of Beatrice's 23rd Armored Division, Phoenix Company, were supposed to be conditioned to bravery, no matter how they felt inside. Never mind that they had the worst record at Fort Chicago for troublemaking, rule breaking, and general hell-raising, they still had a reputation for courage to maintain. Hence Michaels' confident strut into the heart of the Quantum Gate; hence Griffin's mildly startled reaction when the calm voice of an Artificial Person called his name.

"Prepare for Gate Opening," it said evenly. A sexless voice, Griffin noted irrelevantly, and knew that he was grasping at anything to keep from thinking about the Gate, and that high, thin scream. He marched, straight and stiff, into the center of the Gate and stood within the glowing circle, looking back at the faces of the remaining patrol. He wondered if he had looked as nervous as they did now.

The trip from Fort Chicago the night before had been typical military hurry-up-and-wait. The same since the beginning of time, he suspected, whether you were soldiering for God, for Country, or, in this year 2057, for Beatrice International's Military Division, 23rd Armored, owned and operated, trained and staffed by a department of a division of an agency of a branch of one of the world's largest multinational corporations. For the past few years, the 23rd Armored had contracted out to the United Nations.

The platoon had hurried to pack their five-kilo mass allotment, and waited two hours for the transport to show up. They hurried to take their places on board, and waited during the long trip from Fort Chicago. The paint over the window beside Griffin had cracked and peeled, and he perversely stared out at the damaged landscape. Even the laboring, polluted sky looked dirty, and it was impossible to believe that the corrupted soil had ever supported life. No wonder so few windows looked out at the violated land—newer buildings, like this hangar, had no windows at all.

"What?" Michaels had demanded as they came off the transport, gesturing at the huge, featureless hangar. The Artificial Person at the door looked at him with luminous eyes.

"You will be transported via Quantum Gate," the AP, who either could not or would not clarify things, said with mindless friendliness. Quantum Gate? What was that? What did it do? Where would it take them? Griffin listened patiently while Michaels and Alonzo, troublemakers both, peppered the AP with questions, and received no answers at all. But the platoon had speculated, the night before, and thought they knew. The stringent mass allowance and Sergeant Cranshaw's keyed-up excitement seemed to confirm it.

Fort Chicago had a spaceport, Copernicus Station was in the window, and the UN had been upping staff on the orbital since Global Emergency Order 3109 last month. So, they were being sent space-side. What else could it be?

When Michaels asked as much, the AP responded with a friendly smile and shooed them all inside.

But they were all wrong, they had to be. And now Castle and Tisch and Michaels had gone to some unknown place, transported in some unknown way, and Griffin looked at his fellow soldiers and felt sick. Sergeant Cranshaw stared back with her wide, dark eyes. He felt a touch of dizziness and tightened his shoulders even more. He hadn't slept well for the last few nights. None of them had.

The huge gold petals, spread out around him, seemed to quiver slightly. His pulse beat in his throat. The platoon had been told not to eat for twelve hours before this trip, and now he knew why.

Around him, the air began to glow. It was starting. I hope this isn't going to hurt, he thought. As if in mocking answer, the roar suddenly increased, his vision went white, and pain screamed through his body.

A rising column of white bubbles of light pulling him nowhere and everywhere, growing larger and brighter. He was stretched toward every glowing orb and rose through them, torn apart slowly like a sectioned orange, and nothing existed, nothing existed, nothing existed except the pain. He screamed but could not hear himself. He fell upward into nothing. He was dying. He was living five lives. He heard voices, saw flashes of images, and thought the thoughts of other people. And over it, and under it, and through it was stunning, blinding, bright-edged agony.

And then the pain was gone, like a switch clicking off. He had a body, he had a reality. A blurred symbol occupied the center of his vision. He couldn't make his eyes tell him what it was. He didn't care. He was drunkenly delighted to be free of the pain, and back in a place that had a recognizable "where" and "when."

An AP's voice said, "All new arrivals please report to the briefing room in ten minutes."

Terrific. Orders before I can see. Where's the briefing room? Where am I? But the questions weren't that urgent and he smiled, happy to be inside normal military confusion. His vision flickered, then cleared. He was looking at a door. This must be my room. That's a start. He smiled again, tried to move, and passed out.

Chapter Two

Griffin opened his eyes to see a fan set into an oddly angled ceiling. His fingers twitched against the familiar roughness of a military issue blanket—lying in a bunk? Yes, in his billet, in whatever place the Quantum Gate had sent him to. Some Gate, he thought fuzzily. Then he remembered the cool voice of the Artificial Person and the briefing in ten minutes. Ten minutes from when? He blinked—not to worry, the AP would let him know. They were famous for being nosy and intrusive like that.

He sat up too fast, so that his head spun and his vision blurred. He held onto the bunk for a moment, waiting for the dizziness to subside, before carefully swinging his legs out of the bunk. His body felt like it had been taken apart and not put together quite right. Nothing hurt, but the giddiness bothered him. He closed his eyes again and clenched his right hand, driving short nails into the skin of his palm. The pain cleared his head somewhat. He looked around, careful to move his head slowly.

The room was a standard UN enlisted billet. A small table with a chair stood in the center of the room, and a Militerm information terminal glowed from the wall facing him. If he was space-side, it certainly looked no different from any other UN billet he'd seen since enlisting. He grimaced—after all, what did he expect? Little bug-eyed monsters for roommates? He continued his careful survey of the room, and, to his right, saw a shelf piled with the books he'd crammed into his mass allowance.

He raised an eyebrow. This was definitely strange. Since when did privates rate transportation directly into their own rooms? And unpacking services? He sat still for a moment, looking at the three slim books and frowning. No. He had unpacked them himself; he could remember doing it. Gaia, the Gate had a kick like a mule! Was he actually conscious now?

He stood carefully and moved through a short series of wake-up exercises. He kept missing his reach, as though his hands didn't know where the rest of his body was. The feeling dimmed as he ran through the sequence but still bothered him as he walked over the terminal and tapped on the screen.

The message light was on but he ignored it. That pretty much had to be Mom. He selected base maps.

The AP had said the briefing was in ten minutes. He could only hope he hadn't been out for long, or he'd be AWOL from his first orders on the new assignment. The terminal showed him a path from where he was to the briefing room. A couple of halls and one floor away.

Then he asked for a short scan of the entire base, and his breath caught. There were three octagonal floors, each a set of five centers connected by hallways to an inner atrium with elevators. In blueprint, the floors looked like a snowflake. The first floor contained basic operations—the Quantum Gate, security, briefing/simulation, the hangar, and the main entry. A glowing dot showed that he was currently on the second floor, in the enlisted quarters, between a civilian lab and sick bay. The mess hall and a lounge for enlisted personnel were also on this floor. The third floor contained higher-level operations—UN quarters, officers' mess, the commanding officer's quarters, central processing, and UN SciTech quarters.

Griffin let his fingers rest on the terminal screen, staring blankly ahead. The base layout was distinctive and unmistakable—a Class N hardened base, probably part of a cluster or would be soon if it wasn't yet. If the armor was installed, this thing could stand up to a fusion beam. The UN hadn't spent that much money on the new base in Rangoon, where the guerrillas were nearly as well armed as the companies. Where was he that they were blowing *this* kind of money?

His request for a local map got nothing, so he gestured through the whole series of Militerm menus and still couldn't find a map. He folded his arms and stared at the terminal's sketchy menu. Weird. Militerm was always a laugh riot as a data source, but usually there was *something* about the surrounding area. Why would they have omitted that? Maybe they just forgot? Or put up a map and the map crashed?

They had to be at Copernicus Station—they sure as hell weren't at Moonbase, the gravity was all wrong for that, and in all the presumed reaches of the universe, it was the only other place humans could go. And not only was Copernicus a man-made station, and mapped to within a micron, but it was an exclusively UN base. You only got there if the UN meant for you to get there. And once you were there, aside from classified laboratories, every place was accessible—or so the gossip had it.

Space-side meant Copernicus Station.

Didn't it?

An AP appeared in front of him. "General orientation will begin in five minutes. All new personnel to the first-floor briefing room in five minutes."

"OK, OK," he muttered as it vanished. It wouldn't hear him, anyway. He tapped his way back to the main screen and stared at it while his right hand spread over his stomach and he kneaded the muscles, as if he could somehow reach inside himself and get rid of that cold lump of wrongness in his belly. The message light stared back at him.

By habit, he tapped the screen and it listed the calls—only one and sure enough, from his mother. It wouldn't take more than a minute to listen to it, and if nothing else it might distract him, move his mind away from the endless reel of questions, and his body away from that frozen sense of danger. He hesitated a moment longer. According to the map, the briefing room was very close. He tapped the screen again.

The Militerm screen read, "Barbara Griffin, 11/25/57, 170 seconds."

"Run it," said Griffin and pulled the chair to face the terminal.

She held out a remote as the picture flared into view on the wall. Her soft face was determined and her hair was carefully arranged. She wore a suit, had a flower in her lapel, and all the pictures on the wall behind her were straight. Griffin shook his head at the screen and felt a stab of unwanted sympathy for her. She had dressed up to make the vid-letter! She tried so hard. She always had. Suddenly he forgot the cold spot in his stomach and leaned forward, intent on the image of his mother and the years of history and habit and responses that made up their relationship. Yeah, Mom always tried so damned hard.

"Hi, Drew, sweetie, it's me. I hope you're well. It's so funny to be talking to you like this. I hope you know what you're doing."

Griffin grunted, glad she couldn't see or hear him. Since when did his mother *ever* think he knew what he was doing? Jenny had said—Griffin shook his head. Don't think about Jenny.

"I . . . we're all well here. Betsy and JoJo say 'Hi.' They have a friend who's at Fort Bragg. It is funny to be talking like this. 'Where's he stationed?' Stuff like that. I never thought I'd end up a military mom."

She looked down. He couldn't see her lap, but he knew she was wringing her hands, the way she always did when she was upset. She looked up and the careful smile had dropped, leaving confusion and anger naked on her face. "Oh, damn it, Drew, I can't believe you just ran off and joined the God-damned army!"

The outburst surprised a laugh out of him. He hadn't expected her to be that honest. That's part of why he'd refused direct contact for so long—he just couldn't stand the thought of watching her try to pretend she wasn't upset about his enlistment.

She was embarrassed. "I'm sorry. I swore that I

wouldn't swear. It's your life and . . . I just love you, son, and I hope you're all right."

"I love you, too, Mom," said Griffin into the empty room, his voice choked. "But I sure wish you would give up on me."

"I have a rally tomorrow. It's going well. I think it is, anyway. It's so hard to tell what's really going on these days. You know these men, at the UN and the Congress, they'll tell you anything to your face and turn right around and . . . oh, I don't know. It doesn't matter."

Doesn't matter? Griffin felt chilled. She had always insisted that even the smallest green action mattered. Pick up a plastic bag off the sidewalk and get it into the recycling program instead of into a landfill—everything mattered.

The only person he'd met who even came close to her dedication was Private Tisch, the heavyset Green fanatic in the platoon. Tisch believed that only the UN, as a planetary organization, had a chance of staving off catastrophe. Barbara Griffin wasn't quite that fanatical—and nowhere near as convinced of either the UN's power or its benevolence.

But like Tisch, Barbara Griffin persisted. That was her most fundamental characteristic. His father had said, "People look at Barbara's baby face and they think they can squash her. But she just keeps coming back, doesn't she?" Dad hadn't much cared for

Mom's causes, yet he had a grudging respect for his wife's determination. Even as the planet poisoned around them, as the problem got bigger and more out of control, Barbara Griffin persisted in insisting that each tiny gesture made a difference, each little motion counted. Her stubborn bravery made her son want to cry, or strangle her, or both.

But this wasn't the first time she'd said such a thing, was it? The last year or so she had continued her activism as vigorously as ever, but she had begun making sad remarks about whether any of it could really make a difference.

He'd noticed, but hadn't really thought about it. He had been too busy fighting with Jenny and not quite failing medical school.

"Anyway, look. How is it there? I'm dying to know what army life is like. The other night your Aunt Jane and I downloaded this new Patrick Stallone movie where he's in the army—we couldn't figure out the interface—it had all these switches and stuff—anyway, it was all so rough. Do they really fight like that in the army? I hope you're not fighting like in that movie; all they did was fight."

"Oh, fer crying out loud, Mom," said Griffin.

"Oh, fiddle. I'm out of time. All right, real quick." Barbara Griffin took a deep breath and looked into her recorder.

"I saw Jenny yesterday. She's doing good. She sends her love and . . . she says that she'll be calling you soon. I thought maybe I should warn you. Anyway, son, I love—"

The screen went blank.

Griffin felt hair rise on his arms. Jenny might send him a message? Lovely, laughing, broken Jenny—oh Gaia, please, no.

She was the reason he had joined the army, far older than the other new recruits. She was the reason he had run away, one more time, the last in what seemed to him to be a long, long series of departures. Pretty, pretty Jenny, who would never be pretty Jenny again.

He slapped the terminal off and flung himself toward the door. Running away again, and he knew it.

Chapter Three

The door of his room smoothly irised open as he approached, revealing a small entryway bordered by several doors like his own. The floor was undecorated Spectrastone, the structural cross-hatching clearly visible.

He scanned the names on the nearest doors. Michaels, Whalen, Alvarez: looked like the rest of the platoon was billeted here. Good. None of the doors were open, and he decided not to bother querying them. He didn't feel much like talking to anyone right now—especially Michaels, who would have some cockeyed paranoid theories about the Gate, and wherever they were now, and anything else that had caught the man's fancy. Increasingly, Griffin didn't entirely discount Michaels' theories—it was just that he preferred, on the whole, to try to puzzle things out on his own.

His footsteps echoed as he walked across the dark floor. The exit opened ahead of him and he entered a long curving corridor, with the lift entrance in front of him. Jenny wouldn't like this place. She would say it hadn't been made for humans. She would be right. Most military bases weren't.

Jenny. Maybe it was the Gate and whatever it had done to him, but he had lost the ability to think about something else when her name crossed his mind. Jenny. The word rang in his brain, and he shook his head, then had to stop for a moment as his queasy body threatened to rebel.

After a moment, things quieted down and he forced himself forward, through a gold and gray hall that led to another door and into the lift. The door closed behind him and he stopped, startled by bright green foliage and flowers after the darkness of the halls. He was in a glass tube clinging to the circular wall of a three-story atrium. Clear light shone from a faceted source near the top. A spiral of lights wound through the center from top to bottom. The density and richness of the greenery was impressive. He took a minute longer, just looking. Sealed cities were more and more common on Earth, and each sealed city had its hydroponic gardens that generated not only food but the very air the citizens breathed. But this didn't look like the usual cabbages-and-peas civic garden—this looked free and wild and bright, like something out of a storyvid—a history show, or a fantasy. It looked so natural that he thought it might even rain in there, sometimes. Clear, bright, fresh rain. How much water did it take to maintain that?

He pressed the button for the first floor, and watched the atrium change as the lift lowered him. At the bottom, a replica of the Venus de Milo stood in the center of the greenery, womanly curves glowing in the light. He suddenly remembered Jenny's tapestry, green and naked and glowing.

Angrily, he pushed the thought away. Jenny was the past, as much past as free-running water and green trees—just a fantasy. He strode down the hall and through a door labeled "Briefing/Simulation," wishing he could find an old-fashioned hinged door so he could slam it.

The briefing room was surprisingly small, capable of holding maybe fifty people at most. Fewer than twenty milled around, amid a low murmur of voices. An unknown red leaf symbol decorated the far wall; to his right hung a huge poster emblazoned with the words "Eden on Earth." He wondered vaguely what that was about as he sat down. The wall facing him was a 3D viewscreen, now whited out.

The platoon's voices seemed muted, as though everyone was feeling a bit strange. He cradled his forehead in his hands and looked at his mates from under the tent of his palms. Sergeant Cranshaw stood on the far side of the room, talking with a tall man in a UN lieutenant's uniform. Did that mean they'd be working closely with the UN? Great. The lieutenant looked even more ironside than most.

Michaels lounged in his seat, looking around the briefing room as though waiting for a reason to object. He'd find one soon enough—he always did. Nearby, Hawkins sat neatly, hands steepled together. Probably giving thanks for his safe arrival, Griffin thought without sarcasm. Scuttlebutt had it that Hawkins had once been a minister, until discovered to be helping himself to the offerings plate. Nobody had asked Hawkins about it, though—the man had an air of deep and quiet dignity, and even in the short time Griffin had known him, Hawkins had functioned as the platoon's counselor and confessor.

Hotpants Hynick occupied a seat near the door. Youngest in the platoon, he was also hands-down the single horniest human being Griffin had ever known. The platoon was of the collective belief that Hynick, given the appropriate encouragement, would hump anything that moved and a few things that didn't. So far, the lanky country boy had done nothing to change this opinion.

Private Castle's empty hands moved through the air, shuffling an invisible deck. She'd been transferred out of previous platoons for gambling—or, more particularly, for winning. In fact, there wasn't a member of Phoenix Company who hadn't served time elsewhere and been booted out—except for Andrew Griffin himself. The new kid on the block. He would have been tempted to tell himself that he'd been slotted into the platoon only to make up the numbers, but deep inside, he knew better. He'd spent most of his life running away from one thing or another. Joining Beatrice was simply the last in a long line of getaway attempts.

His head swirled again, sick and dizzy, and he gripped the edges of the table in front of him. This feeling of sickness had to be because of the Gate, he thought. And the tension, and the lack of good sleep. Either that, or he was finally losing his mind. He leaned back and closed his eyes, and memory assaulted him.

Mother was turning toward him as he walked into her living room. She looked worried and old. "Drew—there's been an accident."

Her face dissolved into Jenny's tapestry. Jenny had spent nearly a month's wages on the reproduction and installed it on the wall above her bed. What was its name? Bright colors. Naked people dancing in a circle, a deer wandering nearby.

The sound of rushing water.

Shining in bright light, Jenny pranced through the orchard. The unruly mane of her soft curly hair drew his eyes and his hands. He'd been reluctant to take the trip, worried about the time off from studying and daunted by the greenhouse's visiting fees. Now he was in a daze of love and joy as he watched her delight in the growing plants. She plucked a ripe peach, bit into it, and then smiled as though she had invented the glorious taste right there.

She was so beautiful! Looking into her eyes was almost unbearable, looking away was worse. He reached for her, folded her warm soft body against his, felt her arms encircle his waist. Deep inside him, a silent voice was saying, "Jenny, angel, perfect angel, don't leave me. Please don't ever leave me. I can't be without you." He loved her so intensely it frightened him. He didn't know what to do with the feeling, what it meant, how he could live with it.

He kissed her, the peach taste still strong in her mouth, and he tasted peach from her lips, murmuring "Marry me, Jenny, marry me, marry me, I'll never leave, I love you so much, I'll never leave you, marry me, Jenny, I love you." And Jenny said, "Yes, yes—I will." And she reached for him again.

He heard sirens wailing. The rising sound overlaid her beloved face. He tried to hold on to her. She was slipping away. She looked at him sadly. No, don't go, stay with me, never. . . .

✧ ✧ ✧

"Griffin!"

Griffin's eyes popped open. A sharp-faced man with a tidy black beard was glaring at him. Dark eyes bored into him from under a widow's peak that was as sharply pointed as a lance. Griffin blinked in confusion. What had he done to incur the wrath of this man?

"Private Griffin, might I suggest you confine your sleeping activities to your off-duty hours?"

The man wore a black jacket with gold braid and gold edging on the collar. A red collar crowned his snowy white shirt. A UN colonel. Ah, hell. Must be his new C.O., Saunders. Great first impression he'd just made.

"Yes, sir. Sorry, sir," he said and sat up straight.

Michaels cracked up. Hawkins was doing a better job of hiding it, but his shoulders were shaking, and Sergeant Cranshaw's glare was as cold as the colonel's. Griffin felt his face redden as he looked back at Saunders. He had never fallen asleep like that before, never had daydreams of such overwhelming intensity. What was happening to him?

The colonel's rock-hard dark eyes held him a moment longer, then released him and scanned the rest of the room. The laughter stopped abruptly. Griffin took a deep breath. Whatever it was, it would have to wait. Maybe he'd see the medic later.

"Now then," said Saunders, "if we can proceed without further disturbance to Private Griffin," another sharp glance sliced into him, "might I point out that we are here under the auspices of United Nations Global Emergency Order 3109. Our mission here is of the highest priority and is top secret. The policy shack at the UN has instructed me to protect the status of this mission with extreme prejudice."

He paused, then said, "All aspects of this operation are governed by the International Indentured Forces Act. So, we don't have to worry about a repeat of the . . ." Saunders paused, smiled grimly, and his gaze swept the room again. "Unpleasantness in Rangoon."

Griffin's jaw slackened. Indentured! The only difference between military indenture and outright slavery was that the military, usually, paid you. And "extreme prejudice" simply meant that the UN had every right to slaughter you, if they thought it suited their purposes, if they felt it fulfilled the mission. What had Beatrice International sold them into now? The "unpleasantness in Rangoon" had been a full-scale rebellion. The threat couldn't have been more plain if Saunders had pointed a weapon at them.

He glanced down the room at the rest of the platoon, all of whom looked as grim as Griffin felt. The dizziness didn't go away, but the ice in his stomach grew.

Saunders gestured toward two women on his left,

introducing them as Dr. Elizabeth Marks and Dr. X. I. Li, her assistant. Dr. Li was a short, elegant-looking woman who appeared to be part Caucasian and part Asian. She was completely overshadowed by Dr. Marks who, despite a very severe hairstyle, had a compellingly female presence. She looked to be in her late forties, far older than the women who usually drew his gaze, and she seemed very tense. Dr. Marks moved like a woman who knew her own body. Jenny might have moved that way when she was older, but the accident changed that.

No! Stop thinking about Jenny. Pay attention!

Dr. Marks nodded at Saunders and Griffin suddenly leaned forward, paying attention so deep it was almost painful, thirsty to learn anything and everything that would help him understand where he was, and why he was here, and how he could possibly hope to get out with his skin intact.

Chapter Four

I'm sure it will come as no surprise to anyone here that the Earth is on the verge of environmental Armageddon." Griffin blinked. Usually civilian types eased into talks, but Dr. Elizabeth Marks faced the platoon and rapped out the words as though they hurt her mouth.

Private Michaels, ever the troublemaker, lounged back and said, "You been watching ICCN, uh, Doc?" He would get even for being indentured with extreme prejudice, no matter what it took.

Sarge cut in, "That'll be quite enough out of you, Michaels."

Dr. Marks looked at Michaels as if he was a rather uninteresting wart. "Actually, soldier, ICCN's coverage leaves a bit to be desired. The situation is much worse than any of you have been led to believe."

24

Much worse, thought Griffin, how could it be much worse? Kansas, Iowa, Illinois, and Indiana on fire; one of the world's greatest industrial powers besieged by "unpleasantness"; and a third of the world population suffering from Chronic Water Deprivation Syndrome?

The doctor's face looked back at them. Suddenly, Griffin believed her. Not bad, not worse, but *much* worse. For an instant, Griffin didn't want to know, didn't think he could handle knowing.

Dr. Marks nodded grimly, as though she could read his thoughts. "The Environmental Emergency Management Office estimates that irreversible cellular death of the Earth's ecosphere will begin in less than five years."

Five years? That just couldn't be. His mother's Green groups had access to an amazing array of computer equipment and technical knowledge. Papa Maynard alone was worth ten normal AIs since it had decided on manumission. The worst it had forecast was Gaia death in fifty years, which was still pretty serious. Griffin could understand how the UN might have data that the old AI couldn't ferret out, but how could it be an order of magnitude off?

Dr. Marks turned to face the 3D screen behind her and called out. A moment later the briefing room darkened and the round orb of a cartoonishly yellow sun glowed into life. Clouds swirled around it and blue text scrolled in front of the holographic images. A female voice that seemed to form inside his head read out the words.

"Clouds hid the sun, and the hand of man withered on its rod. The beasts of the field fell into pits and holes and the smoke from all the world's burning made our eyes water. Ancient Sumerian Text."

Billowing dark clouds closed in around the sun like the shutting of a gate. The faint figure of a man looked at his malformed hand while a sheep bawled. The scene faded to black as the text shifted to red.

Griffin frowned. What did this have to do with a UN mission?

In rolling phrases, over a background of shanty towns, rusting machinery, and old highways, the voice outlined the history of Earth's illness, the death by poison of rivers and forests and plains. "EEMO's massive neural super-computer, after four and a half years of intensive computation on the WORLD-Five simulation model, has projected 2062 as the year when the Earth's environmental decline can no longer be reversed."

Griffin stared, and the Artificial Person solemnly told him that, by the year 2084, the irreversible process would be completed. And there it was, bleak and hard and naked for all the world to see—the death of the planet they called home, sooner even than the Green's most hysterical predictions had forecast.

"I knew it," Tisch muttered angrily behind him. "I knew it was bad, I knew someone was lying—"

"Can it," Sarge's voice said, quietly but with absolute firmness, and Tisch subsided.

The 3-vid image faded into a picture of Dr. Marks, and Griffin heard Michaels snort angrily. They'd actually had the gall to depict Marks with a *halo* behind her head.

A new voice spoke. "Enter Dr. Elizabeth Marks and Dr. Vi Rampajni. While at Beatrice's Particle Accelerator Laboratory, Dr. Marks created a 'Quantum Gate'—a device that was capable of reaching into the parallel reality frequencies surrounding our own."

Dr. Marks's face was replaced by shifting images of an immense electrical generator, and a machine that flashed and simmered with light.

"However, the device's gargantuan energy requirements and the huge amounts of toxic waste it produced rendered it useless for any practical application."

The head and shoulders of a dapper Asian man appeared on the screen. He did not have a halo.

"Dr. Rampajni," said the AP, "is best known for his work with iridium dioxide—perfecting 'fusion washing,' a technique that produces huge amounts of oxygen, water, and ozone." Molecules danced through the air in front of him, looking as though he might be able to capture one in his hand. "Iridium dioxide's extreme rarity rendered this promising technique nothing more than a laboratory novelty." The scene closed up, and Dr. Rampajni's hologram shrank until it had vanished.

Another Artificial Person appeared, a Caucasian woman this time. "One day," she said, and the date "11/25/47" scrolled past in large numerals behind her head, "fate would intervene and bring these two world-class scientists directly into each other's path. While trolling quantum locations, Dr. Marks discovered Planet AJ3905: a medium-size class A planet with huge reserves of iridium dioxide. The Eden Project was born."

And the Eden Project, according to the words on the screen, was a United Nations Security Program, Classification A1, Top Secret. Griffin wasn't the only one who groaned. People got shot just for knowing there was such a thing as A1 stuff. It didn't help to realize that this classification was why they had been indentured. He took a deep breath and argued with the fear. The UN wouldn't pay "gargantuan" energy costs and create masses of pollution shipping out a bunch of grunts just for the pleasure of killing them. Pay attention. Do what you're told.

The AP told them that all kinds of multinationals, both governmental and corporate, had an interest in the Eden Project, and it said that Eden's goal was to buy time, to give Earth's leaders a chance to find a solution before the planet's ultimate death. First, the AP said, would be the creation of an iridium dioxide mining outpost on Planet AJ3905.

The image of a yellow-green planet with large black areas appeared, and a white circle formed around a small section. The circled area expanded. The name "Johnson's Archipelago" appeared below it.

Griffin looked at the largish island off the coast of a continent. Is that where they were, on an archipelago of a different planet? Amazing.

"And second, the construction of multiple high-capacity fusion scrubber sites around the globe." The map of Earth suddenly blossomed with small red dots. "Iridium dioxide will be harvested on AJ3905, transported through the Gate, and processed on Earth."

The view changed to one of a camera looking up into a sunlit blue sky through leafy trees.

The three AP voice combined into a chorus: "Let the sweet waters pour forth, nourishing beasts and men."

Next to him, Griffin heard Michaels gag. Sweet and holy Gaia on a crutch, Griffin thought in amazement, as the lights came up. We're in freakin' outer space.

Chapter Five

D r. Marks stood silently at the front of the room for a moment, looking at them. No one spoke, no one even moved. She swallowed. "As you can see, this couldn't be more important."

Griffin stared at her. I guess not!

"Literally the future of our race is at stake here." She looked up and then closed her eyes. When she opened them again, fear and pain shone from her face. "We've really screwed this up. You know, at the end of the twentieth century, most of the world's scientists signed an open letter to humanity saying we felt that without significant effort the Earth's ability to sustain life would be severely jeopardized."

She blinked rapidly and her voice shook. Saunders took a step toward her. "The world's governments ignored our pleas and now they are asking me to—"

Saunders stepped forward and raised his hand as though he was going to touch her shoulder. Griffin had the impression that he might have if other people hadn't been watching.

"Dr. Marks!" he said sharply. "Let's stick to the subject at hand."

Dr. Marks glanced at Saunders, started to speak, then shook her head. She strode off the platform, Dr. Li, her assistant, following closely.

After a moment, Saunders cleared his throat. "Now, on to some specifics. All the lead officers here are regular UN as are the SciTechs and the technical contractors. The first group of coalition forces was from the EC 3rd Airborne Division. Our latest addition has been Beatrice's 23rd Armored Division and I have received information that the next Gate opening will bring us a division of MBM's Elite Guard."

Griffin exchanged cynical glances with Michaels. The Elite Guard were rumored to be the biggest heavies in the entire military, a tough, seasoned, and ruthless group of fighters. The 3rd Airborne were no slouches, either. So what was Phoenix Company, known fuck-ups, doing in company like that?

"So who says those guys are so hot?" Michaels whispered. Griffin tried to ignore him.

"So, as you can see, the entire international community is lending the UN its full support. Now, then, does anyone have any questions?"

Whalen raised her hand, and Saunders nodded. "Why is there such a large military force here for just a mining operation?"

"The surface of AJ3905 is toxic so the duty will not be without its hazards."

Griffin raised his hand. "So, why is this mission top secret?"

"The UN is very concerned about creating a global panic. Obviously nothing is to be gained from that kind of chaos. But rest assured that all the appropriate national and corporate forces have been advised of the situation."

Griffin did his best to keep his face blank. Global panic? Everyone knew the Earth was suffering—if you told them you were mining for a solution, what possible panic could there be? Just don't tell people about the terrible countdown, the closeness of planetary death—then Griffin shook his head angrily. Am I supposed to think those people care about anything but their own profits and hides? Aren't they the ones who created this mess? And why would they tell *us* the truth? It just didn't make sense.

Hawkins gestured for attention and Saunders nodded. "What's the time frame for completion here?"

"The Eden initiative will continue for at least several decades and it might even prove viable as a long-term solution to the Earth's environmental situation."

Michaels raised his hand. Saunders stared at him. Michaels said, with his face as straight as a child's, "What's for lunch?"

Griffin would have laughed if he hadn't thought Michaels was being stupid. Saunders did not look like someone to mess with.

Saunders said, "I believe it's bratwurst, Private Michaels." Michaels nodded and smiled happily, his ears sticking out like handles on either side of his naked skull.

Saunders gestured to his left, "Lieutenant Andrews, will you finish up here?" and then walked out of the room. Griffin thought his next stop would be Dr. Marks. Man, would he love to overhear *that* talk.

Andrews was the dark man Griffin had seen talking with Cranshaw earlier. Must be her counterpart here. Lopez' waving hand caught the lieutenant's attention, and he frowned.

"Yes, Private—ah, Lopez, is it?"

"Yes, sir," Lopez said. "Sir, why are we here?"

Andrews stared at him.

"I mean, we know about the Gate now, and this planet, AJ whatever it is, and all that—but why us grunts? What does the Eden Project need soldiers for, sir?" Lopez gestured with both arms, as if to include every soldier in the room. "Why are *we* here?"

Andrews looked at Sergeant Cranshaw, who nodded her head sharply, once, and stepped forward to face her platoon.

"Fair enough, Lopez," she said evenly. "We're soldiers. Our mission is to protect this station and the mining outpost. That's why we're here."

Private Whalen raised her hand. "OK," she said. "Protect them against what? We're on another planet, there shouldn't be any rebels here."

Cranshaw favored her with a tight, lopsided smile. Whalen didn't smile back.

"Absolutely correct, Private," the sergeant said. "There are hostile natives here. The bugs are about three meters tall, have a lot of arms and legs, and can jump like you wouldn't believe. You'll learn all about them in about thirty minutes. In the meantime, fall out."

Chapter Six

"Oh, man," Alvarez said with disgust. "Bugs? I freakin' hate bugs."

The platoon had moved to the enlisted lounge on the second floor and now sat huddled around a large table, bent toward each other, bodies tense and faces stiff.

"She's gotta be joking," Whalen said. "Three meters? That's nuts, just plain nuts. I don't believe it."

"Yeah, well, I do," Michaels said, looking disgusted. "And it's gotta be dangerous, too. Something about it, bugs or weapons or this planet, something's deadly about this stuff."

Tisch raised his head. "Not necessarily. You saw that video—this is a whole new planet. There's no way of telling what's out there. Us, we're trained to be alert, to be quick, to pay attention, to defend—"

Alonzo hooted. "Us? Alert, quick—shit, whatever you're on, man, I want some of it."

"Don't be an idiot," Tisch retorted. "Sure, we're not your usual company, and sure, we've got more than our share of people who got kicked out of other platoons—"

"Nobody kicked *me* out," Alvarez said complacently. "I left first."

"But if nothing else, we're trained, and when it comes to fighting, we're damned good." Tisch glared at them, and one by one they nodded back. Whatever else Phoenix Company was, they were fine fighting people, and they knew it. Tisch nodded, tightly, and continued, "Hell, if I was on a new planet and didn't know what else was there with me, I'd want me along."

"You and how many Marines?" Lopez responded.

"Don't need any," Alonzo said. "I just figured it out. We're not gonna have to fight 'em—we're just gonna turn Hotpants Hynick loose on 'em."

Castle laughed, and after a moment a few of the others soldiers joined in. Hynick, who thought it was a compliment, laughed loudest.

"OK, OK," Hawkins said. "Bottom line is, we don't know enough yet. So we hang on for another, what, twenty minutes, then the sarge tells us all about it." He stood and stretched. "And in the meantime, I'm gonna find a cup of coffee. Anybody coming along?"

Hynick stood up and followed him out, and the rest of the group broke up. Michaels stayed put, staring glumly at the holographic fake sky covering the walls and ceiling and the unused skyball game that occupied the middle of the room. Griffin, at the far side of the table, watched him surreptitiously and wondered whether Michaels' wild paranoias were as off-the-wall as they sounded.

What had gotten into them, volunteering for a mystery assignment just because Cranshaw said it might be interesting? While the group was waiting for posting, the sarge started talking about some strange information coming out of HQ. She didn't share much about what she had found out, but she said the UN was looking for a new group that could be flexible about their assignment. The higher-ups at Beatrice were also making extraordinary noises about the possibility for promotion and other advancement. She said it had the look of a good deal and she put them in for it.

She was good, Cranshaw. Good and smart and experienced. But she was also profoundly ambitious, something she hadn't bothered to hide. Sergeant Cranshaw looked to be Lieutenant Cranshaw some day soon, and General Cranshaw before she retired. And she was willing, she had said, to take any of them along on the ride with her.

Anyone except, perhaps, Michaels. Michaels was trouble. He'd been in and out of a half-dozen different military outfits, always getting into shit for his big flapping mouth, always able to find a new gig because he was so good with the weapons.

Well, Griffin was a good pilot but he was no marksman and he wasn't a big mouth. He just wanted a place were he could fit in and not have to make decisions anymore. And, he decided suddenly, not have to listen to any more of Michaels' theories. He pushed himself away from the table. The thought of coffee suddenly seemed very good.

But halfway to the mess hall he made a sharp turn and saw Dr. Marks almost running down the corridor. Saunders followed her. He stopped the woman with a hand on her shoulder. She spun around as though uncertain whether to hit him or hug him.

"Beth, what's gotten into you?" The colonel frowned at her. His voice was both kind and impatient.

Dr. Marks's eyes were bright with unshed tears. "I don't know who I am anymore," she said miserably.

Saunders took her by the shoulders and pulled her until she faced him. "We have a job to do. A very important job. A job that our futures depend on." He looked into her eyes, his face softer than Griffin would have thought possible.

She didn't look convinced. "How can you know that what we're doing is right?"

Saunders looked at her with exasperation and something else, something Griffin couldn't quite define.

"Beth," said Saunders, "We've been through this before. What do you want to do? Drag twelve billion people through—"

Griffin must have moved inadvertently, because Saunders saw him and stiffened. He released his grip on Dr. Marks. She looked at him for a second longer, then walked quickly away from both of them.

Saunders fixed Griffin with a frigid gaze and said, "Dismissed, solider."

Griffin stepped toward the mess hall door and it irised open in front on him. Yes, sir. Dismissed, sir. I am out of here. He wondered if Saunders was going to follow Marks, but didn't dare turn around to see.

The Artificial Person in the mess hall cheerfully told him that the twenty-four hour special was bratwurst, which didn't sound at all interesting. Griffin poured himself a cup of coffee and took it to the table where Hynick and Hawkins were lounging over their own cups. Hynick had a familiar look in his eyes, and Hawkins sat with his hand over his brow.

Oh boy, Griffin thought, sitting beside them. Hynick's in love again.

"Private Hynick has a bad, bad sore throat," Hawkins told Griffin sadly. "Poor boy is in pain. Hey,

Griffin, you were a medic—take a look at the kid, will ya?"

Hynick just waved his hand. "Have you seen her, Drew?"

"Who?" Griffin said cautiously.

"The doc—Dr. Mirren. Boy, is she gorgeous."

Hawkins and Griffin exchanged a look.

"Gorgeous, huh?" Griffin said, and sipped at his coffee. He spat it back into the cup, and Hawkins grinned.

"I could have told you that." He gestured at his own, untouched cup. "This has got to be the worst coffee I've had since joining up."

"I mean, she's got these great eyes," Hynick said, oblivious to coffee and conversation both.

"So what're you going to do about it?" Hawkins said. "As if I didn't know."

"I don't know. My throat really hurts a lot, and I don't feel so good anywhere else, either," Hynick said. Griffin wasn't surprised that the kid kept a straight face—Hynick had the ability to buy his own stories lock, stock, and barrel.

Hawkins sighed. "Maybe you'd better see the doc," he said.

"Yeah," Hynick responded. "Yeah, you know, that's a great idea." He jumped up and headed for the door.

"Hey, soldier boy," Griffin called after him, grinning. "The sarge isn't done with us yet, remember?

You'd better check out the doc—I mean, let the doc check you out, later on."

"Oh. Right." Hynick trudged out of sight. Laughing, Hawkins stood.

Griffin thought of telling him about the conversation between Colonel Saunders and Dr. Marks, but for some reason didn't. Perhaps, he thought, because he himself didn't quite know what to make of it yet.

Saunders had said, *drag twelve billion people through*—what? The Quantum Gate?

Twelve billion people was roughly the population of the Earth.

Chapter Seven

The briefing/simulation room had changed. The pew-like benches they'd been sitting on had slid into the walls on either side while a large round platform rose from the center of the room. The simulator bay had five chairs, each facing a monitor.

Sergeant Cranshaw strode forward to take up her position between them and the simulators. She was career military, second generation, and it showed in her economical and confident movements. She was also a fine-looking woman, with dark curling hair and an athletic body. She reminded Griffin of the panther he'd seen stalking a fake jungle at the San Diego zoo, and nearly everyone in the platoon had indulged in highly nonmilitary thoughts about her from time to time. She knew it, but no one ever got under her guard.

She exchanged a few quiet words with Lieutenant Andrews as the set-up change to simulation bays completed, then he left and she looked at her platoon. They quieted immediately.

"We'll be taking a look at all the battlefield and VR procedures," she said. "So, pay close attention because this stuff is mission critical. Your lives will depend on it. The atmosphere of AJ3905 uses chlorine like ours uses oxygen, and it's got enough organic hydrocarbons and fluorine compounds floating around in it to eat your brain while it eats your face. We're using standard CO atmosphere suits. They're fitted with—"

Michaels broke in. "Just CO suits? That's bullshit. Why don't we get some augmentation? COs have no armor value at all."

Griffin rolled his eyes, but Alonzo leaned forward, ready to back Michaels up. And when, Griffin reminded himself, had Michaels ever been wrong about an equipment issue? The man was a flapmouth, but when it came to the tools of his trade, there was nobody better in the platoon. Including, perhaps, Sergeant Cranshaw.

"Sorry, Michaels. You're right, but I don't have the answer."

"Well, maybe you should find out, Sarge." Michaels crossed his arms.

"Yeah? And maybe you should shut your wordhole."

Alvarez laughed, but Michaels just looked superior.

"I *have* made inquiries, Private Michaels," Sarge replied, "because it is important to me to keep my boys happy and healthy so that when they return from the battlefield they can service me in the fashion to which I have grown accustomed." She winked and Griffin saw Whalen grinning at Hynick, who turned both pink and avid. In your dreams, boy, only in your dreams.

"But my superiors in the UN have informed me that Beatrice's 23rd Armored does not call the shots around here." She raised an eyebrow at Michaels as though to ask if he thought they did.

"The CO suits, inadequate as they may be, have been retro'd with the latest VR augmentation TopHats. Absolutely state of the art. Complete heads-up. Computer-assisted targeting and ranging. Complete window-in-a-window top-down of the combat zone. Cerebral Cortex transmission coil so the response time is very good."

Michaels interrupted again. "We used those helmets in Belgium. They suck. I had a migraine for a week."

Sarge looked at him. "Private Michaels, are you an expert in freaking everything?"

Michaels gave her the happy grin of a proud two-year-old. "Uh, yeah, Sarge, pretty much I guess I am."

"I find this very hard to believe." She pinned her

black-eyed gaze on Griffin. "Private Griffin, do you think that Michaels is an expert on freaking everything?"

Griffin squirmed. No right answers here. "No, Sarge. I thought that was you." He smiled weakly at her, hoping she would see the ingratiating reply as a joke.

Sarge nodded. "That's correct. I *do* know freaking everything. I know, for instance, that you and Private Michaels for the rest of the week are going to be pulling KP duty."

"Come on Sarge," said Griffin. "I didn't do anything."

"Don't whine, soldier. It's very unbecoming." She arched an eyebrow at him.

Griffin opened his hands in defeat. Yeah, and getting covered with veggie machine muck was becoming? When was the last time *you* did it?

Sarge smiled as though she could read his thoughts, and moved on with her briefing. "Exposure to the atmosphere of AJ3905 is extremely hazardous. The docs call it 'profoundly damaging.' The effects are violent, painful, difficult to treat, and irreversible. Any breach of the CO suit would prove catastrophic." She looked each member of the platoon in the face. "So, ladies, let's not get a run in your stockings."

Michaels said, "Which is why we need something a little warmer on than just a CO suit."

Hawkins burst out with, "Man, I wish you would give it a rest." Griffin flinched. What was it about Michaels that made it so easy for him to rile Hawkins who was normally so calm.

"Why don't you go flatline?" Michaels glared at Hawkins, and clenched his right fist.

Hawkins started toward him, but Cranshaw stopped him with a short chopping gesture.

"Michaels, don't piss me off. We're through with that one."

Cranshaw looked at him steadily, her face not even angry as she waited to see what he would do. She didn't overtly move into either an attack or a defense posture, but something about the way she held herself reminded Griffin of her hand-to-hand combat prizes. Platoon rumor, which she neither confirmed nor denied, said that Sergeant Cranshaw hadn't lost a match in over eight years. Griffin had once watched her take down a guy twice her size when she was so drunk she could barely stand.

Michaels looked back at her for a long beat. Then he crossed his arms and leaned back. Griffin wasn't the only platoon member who remembered to breathe in that moment.

Sarge continued as though nothing had been said. "The VR in the TopHats is keyed into brain wave and retinal activity, so it's the next best thing to being there. Targeting is handled automatically—just look and lock. So, everybody step up to the simulator bay.

"We've got five seats in the bay, so we'll be doing the runs with half the platoon at a time. Your training schedule has already been posted on Militerm. Check it after you leave. Don't make me come after you, or you'll have a rough session."

She smiled, and Griffin remembered a past training run with a shudder. Cranshaw never held grudges, but if she didn't like what you did, she made sure you didn't like the consequences.

"The UN wants us to spend at least two hours a day either in VR or on missions."

"Two *hours*? What is this crap?" Michaels again, of course. "We've been in training for months. We know the suits, we know the skivvers. Why spend so much time zombified under a TopHat?"

"I know that's unusual, but keep in mind it is mighty freaking unusual to be on an alien planet. You'll be grateful for the training after the first bug attack. The UN has already been here for months, and they know what they're doing with this schedule."

"Well, I just hope sick bay won't be stingy with the pain killers when I get my next migraine."

"Aw, poor baby's little head might hurt?" said Castle, and a snicker ran through the group.

"*You* ever had a migraine?"

"Every month, baby boy."

"Knock it off, folks," said Cranshaw. "Migraines

can indeed be a side effect of cortical stimulation. However, I'm sure you'll find the UN has improved the process vastly in the past year." She looked at Michaels. "And I am also sure Dr. Mirren will be happy to soothe your fevered brow if you ask her nicely."

Another laugh swept the group, and Michaels joined in. His success with the ladies was sometimes resented and sometimes admired within the platoon. Castle claimed to have followed him around one evening, taking notes and trying to figure out how he did it. She joked about selective projective telepathy, which Griffin almost believed, having watched Michaels in action himself. Michaels said it was just paying attention, but that hadn't ever worked for Griffin.

"Now, sessions will be at least an hour long, and sometimes the full two hours. It depends on whether you make me happy with your performance. The first group to go will be Michaels, Hynick, Griffin, Lopez, and Hawkins. Tisch, Alvarez, Whalen, Alonzo, and Castle—you'll be next. You are at liberty until thirteen-hundred hours. Check out the base if you want, but keep in mind this is a high-security mission and many areas are off limits. You can also passively observe sim runs via Militerm. Or you can pass the time with Castle's mass allowance."

Cranshaw grinned and Castle winked. Castle had

a passion for poker. Gambling was technically banned on bases, but Cranshaw didn't much care if they kept the ante and the noise down.

"One more thing—there's a welcoming reception at nineteen-hundred. Wear your dress uniform." The group groaned. "Knock it off, folks. You don't need to stay long. OK, now you five take your seats and the rest of you try to stay out of trouble."

Chapter Eight

Tisch and the others left, while the remainder fanned out around the sim bay. The chairs were spare but surprisingly comfortable. Griffin's screen in front of him said, "VR Display Systems" in blue letters against black. Oh, goodie. Video games. He tapped the keyboard and a TopHat slid over his head.

He'd worn one before, but only for a few minutes at a time. They made keyboards and display screens, even 3D screens, completely superfluous. The intensity of the virtual reality was amazingly vivid, but he purely hated the first ten seconds. The helmet's connectors tickled through his scalp and he knew that almost microscopic threads were piercing his skull. The semi-alive worms would link into his sensory centers, usurping the optic, auditory, and other input nerves. The immense data transmission capacity of the TopHat's connectors would then take over his perceptions. Until the connection was complete, he was in an entirely black world, feeling his sense of touch, smell, hearing, and taste wink out.

The VR software adapted to him and started feeding wait-state signals. He sighed with relief as some sense of having a body returned. He felt more than heard the rest of the platoon find their places and engage. The darkness lighted up with static, then cleared. The run was on.

He had the controls of a skivver under his hands. He was in flight. He grabbed the stick as the nose of his craft started to dip. Woof! This simulation setup sure made you start off fast. Where was he?

The ground underneath was low rolling hills covered with scrubby brown vegetation that was deep black in places. The sky was mostly green but shot through with what looked like jet streams of boiling gold. What were the air currents like up there? He didn't think he wanted to find out.

"Look, everybody stay on your toes."

The ID display said that a Captain Hiaumet was in charge of this sortie. Griffin wondered briefly if there was actually a person of that name on the base, and then he was too deeply into sim to wonder any more. His heart pounded and his breath came fast.

His skivver was hurtling along at over two hundred klicks per hour. Griffin moved up past an approaching hill, trying to maintain an even three hundred meters of altitude. The on-board computer system orders were to stay low in order to spot bugs. Their opponents were good at camouflage and able to fool even the sensors if the distance was over five hundred meters. The roiling gold and green of the sky passed over his head, daunting in its sickly strangeness.

His proximity alarm began to beep and his ship's AP spoke. "Alien proximity alert. No lock available."

Where was it? He scanned but saw only the dark hills and that poisonous sky. The words "Target mode" appeared on the right side of his screen.

"Alien presence. No lock available. Danger."

Yeah, yeah. yeah. Tell me something useful. The beeping of the alarm made his hands shake. Take a deep breath. Focus. Where was the thing?

Movement in the lower right corner of his screen. Yes! Something was moving along the ground, head bobbing, huge faceted eyes, and making a sound like cloth being ripped under water. Gotta be the bug. Gaia, it was ugly!

The targeting square appeared and he tracked in onto the bug. Just as it was about to disappear out the lower left of his screen, he fired. He was sure he'd missed it, but then the bubbling sound shifted to a high grating squeal. Nailed it! His heart rate accelerated with pure joy and he whooped like a toxin siren.

"OK! First kill registered."

"Freaking Michaels?"

Griffin started to answer angrily but the other voice spoke first, "No, Griffin." Yeah, Michaels might be the best shot in the platoon, but he wasn't the only one who could point a weapon around here.

"Mess of bugs in sector Q-A." Griffin swooped down into a valley, feeling high from his kill. Show me those bugs!

Hawkins came on the com line. "I got a skivver strike called in. All Q sector Joes hoof it to quadrant A."

Griffin checked his map. He was in Q-H, headed down line. He pivoted his craft to the right, and another skivver roared past him over his head.

"Squash them bugs!" sang out a voice he couldn't place. Hynick? Was he just looking forward to it or had he actually found some?

Griffin leaned on the throttle and began to move forward again. This thing didn't have much acceleration, did it?

"Alien proximity alert. No lock available."

The skivver that had passed him was now on hover. It began firing into the ground just past the next hill. Griffin once again heard the shrieking sound of a bug's swan song.

"Wiped out that mess!" Definitely Hynick, sounding nearly as high as Griffin had felt a few minutes earlier. How many had he gotten? Well,

Griffin could catch up with the hick boy!

"We're headed for the east quad." East quad? Where was that? Someone had forgotten to use the right coor'd system.

"Jeez! A couple hundred over here. Hundreds!"

That's where Griffin wanted to be! He began to accelerate again.

"Squash them bugs!"

He swung toward the left flank of the next hill a little low to the ground, trying to catch up, and his proximity alarm began that nerve-grating beep again.

"Danger. Alien proximity alert. No lock available." An arrow appeared on his screen, pointing to his right. He pivoted his craft, and saw a huge bug cresting the hill.

"Alien presence. No lock available."

His targeting system came up, forming a red square. He tried to center it on the bug. Fire! The tracer showed a clean miss. The bug was coming at him! He moved his target, fired again, and fired once more. It was so big! How could anything alive be so disgusting? He fired once more and the tracer went underneath the thing as it leapt at him. His screen blasted into static and then went blank.

❖ ❖ ❖

The TopHat lifted off his head, and he leaned back in the chair. He was trembling and he reeked of fear sweat. For a couple of deep breaths, he didn't know where he was. He found himself checking out his body, looking for injuries.

Simulations didn't usually get to him that hard. Those bugs, that sky—Griffin shuddered at the thought of facing those things in real life. The rest of his platoon was still under the simulation, their heads obscured by the TopHats, their hands jerking, and their muffled words occasionally almost audible. He could go into standby mode and watch the run play out.

No. He just wanted to sit quiet and breathe a while.

After about ten minutes, the run was over. Hynick and Lopez had been disabled by bugs, but none of them were rated as kills. So, three team injuries and over 150 bug kills. He glanced at Sergeant Cranshaw. It was her policy to tell them they hadn't done well enough, but he caught a gleam of pride in her eyes before she told them to do another run, and get it right this time.

Griffin leaned forward. His heart began to pound again even before the TopHat had settled over his head.

Chapter Nine

The platoon ran simulations for nearly two hours, and Griffin felt like he had been in the helmet for days. By that time, they were regularly getting kill rates of 400 with no injuries. Even Cranshaw was willing to admit that wasn't bad.

It had been fun. More than fun, really. Griffin was astonished by the intense exaltation of killing those grotesque things. He also felt if he had to make another run he would just plow his simulated skivver straight into a mountain.

"OK, folks," said Sarge. "That's an improvement. Required time for today is now over. Same time, same place tomorrow. If you want added time to practice, the sim bay will be open every day from reveille to lights out, so just check with Militerm and see if it's booked."

Hynick was already on his way out of the room. Lopez and Hawkins stared at Griffin with impatience, evidently planning to go another round, but he pushed his TopHat into the lock mode. The computers could fill in gaps in a platoon with additional simulation, but everyone knew that made the runs more predictable.

He shook his head. He shoved back his chair, stood, and stretched. His reflexes had been OK under sim, but his body still didn't seem to fit right. Neither did his mind—indenture, environmental Armageddon, weird behavior from a top SciTech, and outlandish bugs on an alien planet. Was any of this for real?

He ran his hands over his face and forced himself to move forward. Regs said they were all supposed to report to sick bay within the first twenty-four hours. This seemed like as good a time as any, given how lousy he felt. Maybe the doc had stuff that would help. A nice dose of reality would be fine for starters.

He strode out of the simulation room as though he knew what he was doing and took the lift back to the second floor. Gaia, this place was dark. The only bright spot was the lift atrium. The rest was endless empty corridors with conduits and support girders unmasked and splotches of light marking the doorways. Where were all the people? What were they doing?

He palmed for entry into sick bay and walked into a surprisingly well-equipped miniature hospital. Scanners, PCM, hold booths, and if that projection system was what he thought it was, then he'd never seen better. Impressive. Must be a pleasure to work with such great equipment.

He'd done shifts in an ER during med school but that was in a nearly collapsed section of L.A. Nothing worked except the staff, and most of them looked like they would fall over if they could remember how. This clean and quiet place barely seemed like a medical facility to him.

Hynick was there ahead of him, talking to a woman with an MD caduceus on her uniform. The doctor had soft wild hair, big eyes, full lips, and a body that did amazing things to the standard medical uniform. Woof, damn! Maybe I should mention I was a medical student? Griffin found himself involuntarily giving her a solid up and down look, something that had always bugged him when other guys did it to Jenny. He doubted this lady minded, either. She had at least one more button undone in the front than was needed for comfort.

He crossed his arms and leaned against a wall to watch her.

"All right, soldier," she said to Hynick, "You may put on a robe. They're in the alcove."

Hynick blinked. "Um, you want me to take my clothes off?"

"Yes. Is there a problem?" She was holding a clip-board computer, and looking at him with friendly but tired patience.

"Uh, well, no. No. It's just . . . right here?" He gestured around him, and managed to look both embarrassed and eager.

"No, soldier." She smiled a little. "You may use the examining room." She pointed toward her right.

"Oh. Yeah, sure. Of course."

"Privacy, Bay Two," said the doctor, and an oblong of light and metal extended from above to enclose the examining table.

She turned toward Griffin and gave him a pleasant smile. "All right, soldier. What's your name?"

"Griffin. Andrew Griffin." Her hair fell slightly into her eyes as she bent over her clipboard. He found himself wondering if it was as soft as it looked. That woman just oozed sex. He hadn't had thoughts like this in so long he'd been wondering if he ever would again.

"Marie, status on Griffin."

The nurse, a big, dark woman with "Lukas" on her ID badge, didn't even look up. "He needs to be looked at."

The doctor shook her head. "Do you have that *entire* list memorized?"

"There are only eleven of them. It ain't brain surgery," said the nurse tartly, yet it was easy to see she was pleased. Griffin had a feeling the two had been working together a long time.

The doctor smiled at Griffin and he felt his breathing speed up. Look at that woman's lips! "Good thing for you. Get a robe." She turned toward Bay Two.

Griffin started to watch her walk away but realized the nurse was grinning at him. His ears got hot. He went to a cubicle, pulled the curtains shut behind him, and began taking off his uniform. The flimsy little room was a standard hospital changing room, just like one he and Jenny had occasionally used during medical school.

Making love in a room this small was sometimes more funny than hot. You couldn't lie down and the walls were so flimsy you couldn't lean up against them. They'd struggled to find positions that would work, and struggled even harder not to laugh out loud and call attention to themselves. Griffin smiled at himself in the mirror, seeing Jenny's hair shaking as she giggled.

That was before the arguments started, when things were easy and sweet. They had barely ever even gotten annoyed with each other for nearly a year. It was a joke between them. How could you get mad or stay mad when the sex was so good? One touch and nothing else mattered.

He could remember their first argument so well, too well. You'd think it would have been over something like, "You're not paying enough attention to me." But no. That wasn't Jenny. She was different. She always was. She was the sweetest, smartest woman he had ever met. She was the best lover he'd ever had. She was equally passionate about everything that concerned her. He hadn't realized how many directions that could go.

The game had been due to start in less than five minutes, and he wanted to watch it. He'd known before that she didn't care for football, but that day she'd gotten angry. Very angry.

She wore a white top that was nearly off her shoulders and her soft blond hair was pulled back in a loose knot. The curling tendrils waved gently in the artificial breeze as she leaned against a wall. The screens and machinery of their apartment building's enclosed courtyard made it almost feel like a sunny day outside. The light was a little dim, but they were all getting used to that these days. She was walking away from him as he spoke. He longed to stroke her smooth neck even as his irritation grew.

"What is the big deal about the sticks? They're wearing more padding these days!"

She turned to face him, and her eyes were dark with anger. "It's animalistic. I hate that, Drew." She looked away as though she couldn't stand the sight of him.

"I hate that game and I hate the fact that you *watch* it." Her right hand thudded into her left. "The whole thing was bad enough before, but now they've all these new rules. It's pathetic. And you know what makes it more pathetic? All these people are starting to flock to it."

"Gaia, Jenny. Calm down! It's just a game." Griffin looked at his watch. Three minutes to go.

"This is not a game. Damn it, that's my point." She looked at him with anger and pleading on her face. "You know what I did on my shift last night? I helped a doctor put seventeen staples into a six-year-old's skull. And do you know why? Do you know what happened? His fourteen-year-old brother hit him with a football stick. We're learning how to be doctors, Drew. We're learning how to save people. But we live in a society hooked on violence. And it hurts me to see you become like that."

He'd blown his stack. Even now, he wasn't sure why. Maybe it was just because the game was starting soon and he knew she'd leave if he got angry.

"How can you possibly compare a sport to dumb kids who hurt each other?" he said, the sneer clear in his voice. "I can't believe you're trying to tell me that watching a game is like saying all the bad craziness is OK. Don't you tie me to that! I've had it with people trying to tell me I'm responsible for everything that goes wrong in the world. I'm not, and I *am* going to watch the game."

She hadn't answered. She had just looked at him for a few long seconds, then turned her back and walked away. As he watched her head for the compound's airlock, he almost changed his mind. Almost said, "I'm sorry," almost agreed not to watch the game. This was the finest woman he'd ever met. How could he let her walk away from him? He hesitated, and the airlock had cleared her for exit. The inner door closed. He watched her reclaim her protective gear, and then she was walking down the L.A. street, away from the small apartment they had called home. He hadn't even asked her where she was going or when she would be back.

He turned and went back into their apartment. His team had won.

Griffin carefully hung his uniform on a hook and put on the bright green robe. She had come back and he had apologized, but things between them were injured. He didn't understand it. He hated it. He tried to pretend it wasn't so. It was.

When he pulled aside the cubicle's curtain, the nurse was standing just outside. She batted her eyes at him extravagantly.

"Mmm! That color looks nice on you."

Griffin laughed. "You think so?" he said in a squeaky voice. "I thought it kinda washed me out." She laughed with him, then gestured toward an examining table. He roosted himself on the edge of the table, waiting for the doctor.

The privacy screen rose from Bay Two, where Hynick was being examined. Griffin recognized the machine from medical school—a Jensen Ultra. That's *very* nice.

Hynick was facing the sexy doctor and smiling a shit-eating grin.

"Say Ah," said the doctor and looked into Hynick's mouth.

His old instructor had always said, "Bedside manner can be very important." This doctor had a nice manner, but one that made you want to get into bed with her. Probably not what his instructor meant.

"I don't see any redness or feel any swelling." Her face was sympathetic. Hynick's gaze dropped to her chest. Griffin rolled his eyes, unnoticed by either of them.

"How long has it been bothering you?" she said in a kind voice.

Hynick was still staring at her chest. "Uh, what?" he said.

"I said, How long has it been bothering you?" Her voice was, if anything, still more sympathetic.

"Oh, uh, a couple of days."

"Uh-huh." She used her stylus to make a note on her clipboard.

"What's your first name?"

"Doctor," she said and her smile became positively toothy. Griffin snickered.

"Listen, I just can't see anything. Is it *really* bad?" Her voice dripped with sympathy. Uh oh, Hynick— she is *so* on to you.

"Yeah, it's kinda bad."

"Uh-huh."

"Hey, I hear you're from San Diego."

"You do, do you?" Her smile was as bright as ever, and Griffin tried not to laugh out loud.

"Yeah."

"And where are you from?"

"Tucson."

"Um. Any other symptoms?"

"No, no, just the sore throat."

"Ears bothering you?" She tilted her head, eyes on the private's face.

"No . . . I have an aunt in San Diego."

"Oh, you do, do you?" Still smiling.

"Yeah."

She leaned forward slightly. "Well, I think we should get together sometime and you can tell me all about that."

Hynick had been looking at her chest again. He looked into her face, startled. He smiled like he was a three-year-old who'd just gotten *exactly* what he wanted for Christmas. "Really! Well, uh, I'd like that."

"I'll bet. Marie, would you come in here for a moment, please. Listen, about your sore throat—"

"Oh, it feels better already."

"I'm sure it does, but just to be safe—Marie, five hundred units of B_{12}, please." She faced the private, smiling, ever smiling. Hynick, finally, started to look nervous, and Griffin bit his lip to keep from laughing. "I think you're going to need a shot."

"Oh, man. Not a shot."

"Yes," she said in a slow drawl, "A shot."

"I *hate* shots."

"Yes. I'm sorry, but I think you're going to need a shot. A really *big* shot."

"Can't you do a spray?"

"Sorry, soldier, but this amount of B_{12} can't be administered that way." It was a bald-faced lie, but Hynick didn't know better. She went on, "It won't hurt. Much." She was still smiling, but Hynick wasn't.

The nurse was already there, holding up a syringe the size of a turkey baster. Griffin wrapped his arms around himself, shaking with silent laughter. That was *not* a standard needle.

"Bend over, buttercup," said the nurse, waving her needle.

As Hynick slowly moved into position, the privacy screen came down again. The doctor sauntered over to where Griffin was sitting, looking pleased with herself.

"Privacy, Bay Three." she said, and the barrier slid down around them.

"Hi. I'm Dr. Mirren. Griffin, right?"

"Yes."

"How do you feel, Andrew?"

"I feel fine," he heard himself say in a high voice

and winced at the obvious lie.

"Good. It's just common practice for me to check on all the new arrivals, make sure everything is OK. Sometimes the Gate can make you feel a little woozy for a couple of days. So, just to be sure I'm going to give you a really big shot."

Griffin gaped at her. Oh, no, not a shot!

"No," she said, answering the thought that must have been obvious from his face, and laughed. "Just kidding. But I am going to give you a quick scan."

She gestured toward the control panel to her left and the autodoc field ran down him like a standing wave of light. He felt a flash of warmth and prickles, then the light had passed.

"OK, OK. You're all done." She looked up, and began taking notes of a readout near the top edge of the privacy enclosure.

"Was that a Jensen Ultra?"

She looked surprised. "Yeah. It's nice, isn't it?" Then she nodded. "You were in med school, weren't you?"

"Yeah."

His mother stirring her coffee, looking at him skeptically. "You want to be a neurosurgeon?" She thought neurosurgery was just something he was doing only to please Jenny. Maybe she'd been right.

Of course she'd been right, Griffin thought. And he'd run away from medical school, just as he'd run away from everything else in his life.

Griffin swallowed. "Third year," he told the doctor. Most washouts happened the first year or the last, and he didn't want Dr. Mirren thinking he'd simply failed. Yet, running away was failure, wasn't it?

"U.T., right?"

"Yeah." *Now, how she'd know that? I guess she looked at my file.*

"It's a good school," she said absently, writing down another observation off the Jensen's readouts.

She turned back, and gave him a friendly smile. "A little lunch will probably make you feel a whole lot better. It's just the lag."

Griffin smiled ruefully. *Sure didn't fool her, did I? She* knows *I feel lousy!*

"Listen, if you don't feel better by this afternoon, come see me again."

"So you can give me a shot?"

"A really *big* shot—but only if you want to play games during working hours." She laughed. He raised an eyebrow, thinking about nonworking hours. She winked, and walked away.

He hiked himself down off the table, and walked across the room to change back into his uniform. Hynick was back into his uniform and on his way out, rubbing his butt and looking more confused than pissed. Poor guy still wasn't sure what hit him.

Griffin dumped his hospital gown in the recycler and pulled on his fatigues. As he twitched the curtains aside, he could see the doctor over by the nurse's station, talking to Marie Lukas while she worked at the computer. She waved at him, then said a few inaudible words to Marie. The nurse's grin was vivid against her dark face as she nodded at him on his way out.

Chapter Ten

Griffin found his way to the mess hall. Hynick was complaining to Lopez and Hawkins about his shot. "I tell ya, I won't be able to sit down for a *week*." Griffin could believe it. He covered his smile with a hand and walked quickly toward the mess hall order station. That needle would have been about right for a horse. Dr. Mirren must have special-ordered it. Or maybe it was the nurse's idea—that grin on her face as she had told Hynick to bend over had been pretty impressive.

Griffin got an order of bratwurst from the ridiculously cute mess hall AP, and looked for a place to sit.

Dr. Marks sat alone, staring at a wall. She didn't see him as he approached. She reached into a pocket and pulled out a battered box of cigarettes. Griffin remembered his mother hassling him about smoking, but something more than that made him pause.

They were in a station on an alien planet, he

thought. An alien planet where the atmosphere was highly toxic. Which meant that the station's air couldn't merely be purged and replaced, not even with scrubbed outside air. Which meant that smoking regulations should be identical to the smoking regulations aboard the Copernicus Station, or Moonbase, or any other totally sealed vessel: forbidden. Against regs. But Dr. Marks not only lit her cigarette right there in the public mess hall, but did it in front of a full ashtray.

And Griffin suddenly needed to know why. That, on top of everything else, drove him the remaining meters toward her table, but he stopped again when she looked up at him. She looked pallid, exhausted, and at the end of her rope. He froze, looking at that flat and lovely face, and wanted to reach out for her, take her to sick bay, tuck her into her own bed, do something to relieve the anguish that so obviously lived just below her skin.

"Excuse me. Can I borrow a cigarette?" he blurted out and then flinched inside. Oh, yeah. Smooth way to start a conversation.

She didn't respond immediately, and he almost decided to just slink away and pretend he hadn't said anything. Then she smiled slightly.

"Certainly. Here." She handed him the cigarette she'd just lighted, stood, and left.

Strange. Very strange. He sat down and looked at the cigarette, then stubbed it out, thinking about how she had behaved during the briefing and the conversation he had overheard with Colonel Saunders. This was a lady with trouble on her mind. But what was it? She was going to save the world, her and that fusion-washing process. Seems like she should be very happy.

Maybe she was just upset that the world hadn't wised up sooner. Mom had said much the same, as Marks implied during the briefing, that just a little action fifty years ago would have been a lot better. Hundreds of thousands of species had been lost from the ecosystem in the last hundred years, how many no one would ever know for certain. In the last fifty years, as many humans had died from direct or indirect effects of the ever-increasing pollution. It must hurt to look at that as a scientist and know how unnecessary it all was.

Still thinking about Dr. Marks' odd behavior, Griffin cut off a chunk of bratwurst and bit into it. Then he looked at the remaining piece on his fork in stunned surprise. Good grief—how could you make sausage come out that *dry*? Military food never failed to astonish him. He chewed grimly. Well, Dr. Mirren said food might make him feel better. She hadn't said it needed to be good food. He swallowed the mouthful, chased it with a sip of the dreadful coffee, then dutifully took another bite.

Hynick walked out, and Griffin saw that Lopez had gone to the food control panel. As the large man turned around, holding a tray, Griffin waved to him. He came over and sat down across from Griffin.

"So, Hynick isn't too happy?"

Lopez rolled his eyes.

"I was there when Nursie got out the needle," Griffin continued. "If he told you it was big, he wasn't giving you a line."

Lopez laughed and took a bite of his sandwich, then froze, not even chewing. Griffin laughed.

"Pretty bad, eh?" said Griffin and Lopez nodded. "But it is a perfectly balanced and nutritious meal," Griffin continued in a high sing-song. Hawkins slid his tray onto the table next to them, looked at Lopez' face, and grinned.

Lopez chewed and forced himself to swallow. "Save me from nutrition. Is there *anything* that looks edible around here?"

"Besides the doctor?" said Griffin.

"Is she really that good looking?"

"*Fissionable.*"

"Maybe it's time for my checkup," Hawkins said, still smiling.

"It'll brighten up your day just to see her, let me tell you," Griffin told him. "But don't be out to get anything. She's the kind who smiles sweetly and gets even if you waste her time."

"Hell, I don't want to get anything. Got my honey and my kids back home. But Ellen never made me promise not to *look*. She says if she'd wanted to marry a eunuch she would have found herself one."

Griffin felt his face freeze. Jenny. He'd asked her to marry him, asked her to promise to stay with him always, and the first time she'd had any real trouble, he'd turned and ran. On reflex. Without a word, without looking back.

"Hey, man—you OK?" Lopez was looking at him with concern.

"Yeah, I'm fine. Well, maybe a little woozy. Doc says they call it Gate lag. Maybe I'll see if I can catch a few z's." Griffin stood and picked up his tray.

Hawkins obviously didn't buy the story but he didn't push it either. "You'll sure be needing the beauty sleep. You're on KP all week. Remember?"

"What a friend! Yeah, I remember."

Hawkins started to say something else, then thought better of it. Probably getting set to rag on Michaels. Michaels never hesitated much about trashing Hawkins, but Hawkins pretty much kept his mouth shut once he found out Griffin was friends with him. Jenny had that kind of ethics.

But thinking of Michaels made him think about Michaels' paranoid theories, and he slowly put his tray back and leaned over it. Hawkins was probably the sanest and most stable member of the patrol. The dark man raised his eyebrows and looked at Griffin curiously. Lopez chewed doggedly on his sandwich, watching them both with curiosity.

"Hey, Hawk," Griffin said. "Did you see Doc

Marks smoking in here, earlier?"

Hawkins nodded silently.

"If we're in a sealed station, if the air outside is so damned toxic, then how come she gets away with smoking?"

"She's brass," Hawkins said with a shrug.

"Maybe. But what about how strung out she looks? Or that stuff about indenture? And listen, Hawkins . . ." Griffin leaned forward. "You been sleeping well lately?"

But Hawkins pushed back from the table and stood, shaking his head.

"I don't think about it, and I'm not gonna think about it," he said. "Listen, Griffin, my family needs the money. I signed up for five years and I'll serve them, and I'll be the best goddamned soldier I know how to be. But I'm not buying into any theories, you hear me? I don't ask questions, I just do my job. And in five years, I'm out of here with enough cash to send my kids through school."

He looked at Griffin seriously.

"You do the same, kid. Forget about the crazy stuff and just do your job. It's the only way to go."

Griffin stared after him. He knew it was good advice. He knew that he ought to take it, that a month ago he would have taken it.

And he also knew that, for some reason, this time around, he just couldn't leave well enough alone.

Chapter Eleven

The veggie machine in the kitchen, a gleaming chrome tube, stood at least two meters in diameter and easily four meters long. Standard issue Klaushaut processor, though pretty big for the size of this base. Terrific machines, but why they couldn't have been designed to be self-cleaning was a mystery. Michaels was staring at it in disgust, and a balding man in a cook's uniform stared, in turn, at Michaels. Griffin looked at the man dubiously and winced as Cookie nodded at him. The man did not look sane.

"All right, boys—let's get going. KP is still KP. You know what KP stands for?"

"Keep Peeling," said Griffin.

"That is correct! You're a very smart man," said Cookie. Michaels started grinning. He collected eccentrics, and Griffin could tell that he was about to add a fine specimen to his hoard.

"That machine here—which you two will have

the honor of cleaning—can prepare a full meal for a hundred men in less than an hour. You believe that?" He looked at Griffin intensely, as though the question mattered.

Griffin shrugged. "Yes."

"You do? I don't." He laughed with manic cheerfulness. "When I was on TV . . . Did you know I was on TV?"

"No."

"Me, neither." The cook laughed at his own joke for quite a while, showing large white teeth. Griffin sighed and exchanged glances with Michaels, who looked more and more delighted. The short man calmed himself. "No, no, really. I was on TV. I had my own show. You believe that? I was the star. Interactive Cable Channel 47. Four and a half years I was on that damn show. It was great. I *loved* it. I had a lot of fans. Lots of them."

His eyes gleamed. "Cars. Booze. A house in the Bahamas. Lots of women fans."

Yeah, and they probably just *loved* the way you flipped a crepe.

As if the man had heard Griffin's skeptical thoughts, he stopped suddenly and said, "You believe that?"

This time the cook made the mistake of focusing on Michaels, who looked at him steadily over his folded arms, and said, "No."

The cook's face abruptly turned sad. He said,

"Hey, watch it!" as though Michaels had swatted a fly with a crystal vase. His eyes grew shifty as he searched for another story to tell them, and then he gave up.

"All right, boys. Clean 'er up good," he said curtly and walked away.

Michaels plucked two cleaning rods off the processor's rack and handed one to Griffin with a sardonic smile. A quick twist extended the rod and the glowing ball of the destat field appeared at the end. As Griffin got his going, Michaels went to the far end of the machine and began moving the rod down the side of the machine in steady strokes. Griffin could hear soft thuds from inside the machine as encrusted food paste fell away from the surface.

The trick was to move moderately fast and very smoothly, so the semihardened goo would peel off from inside in one large chunk with each stroke. After they did a pass from the outside, they would have to crawl in and get what remained. A steady hand on the destat could leave the inside nearly as shiny as the outside in one pass.

Michaels was a real expert at KP. By the heavy sound of the falling clumps, he was getting nearly everything. Griffin took up position at the other end of the machine and began scraping, moving toward Michaels. Griffin had gotten a lot more experience at processor cleaning by hanging around with the guy, but it would probably take him years to match Michaels' skill.

The rank smell from the veggie machine filled the air as the charged rods forced paste away from the walls. A veggie machine could turn nearly any organic matter into nearly any kind of food. The food would be perfectly nutritious and individually concocted to suit the metabolism of each person, as recorded during sick bay exams. The problem was getting it to taste like anything but its basic component ingredients.

The Cookie for his last base could pull off that trick. She had an array of flavor and scent bottles which she would snag apparently at random while the machine grunted and hummed, making cheese taste not just like cheese but like Muenster or Swiss. She also knew how to tinker the textures with amazing precision. She could have made mud taste and chew like filet mignon. As he rubbed the machine down, Griffin thought about meals he'd eaten during his Digital Terrorism training, and his mind started drifting until he worked in a blank haze.

A sound penetrated the haze. Griffin blinked, surprised to find his own face, blue eyes too wide and mouth open, staring back at him from the curved side of the veggie machine.

"Griffie? You OK, man?"

Griffin looked at Michaels. Only a few yards separated the two men.

"Uh, yeah, I guess I just, kinda drifted off there." Griffin blinked and shook his head. "I guess I'm still tired. Or whacked out from the Gate. Or something."

"Yeah, or something," Michaels repeated darkly.

"No, don't do it," Griffin said. "I'm tired, man, I'm fried, what ever it is, I don't want to hear about it."

"Come on, man. This . . . this is important. It'll only take a minute." The man's narrow, tough face was serious and Griffin sighed. Michaels took that for assent.

"I don't know what's going on around here, but this stuff they're shoveling isn't going down with just one swallow."

"What are you *talking* about?"

"All this BS about a mining operation. Do you have any idea how much of this stuff it'd take to have any effect on the atmosphere?"

"Huh! I didn't know you had a degree in geo-engineering." Griffin started working again, making more noise than necessary.

"You don't have to be a rocket scientist to figure this stuff out. I was talking to the mechanic earlier." Michaels paused, and leaned against his scraper. "There's only one mechanic here. In the whole damn motor pool there's only *one* mechanic. They're gonna dig up enough of this ore to fix the entire planet and there's only one mechanic here?"

Michaels looked at Griffin, his face angry and tense. Reflexively, Griffin stopped scraping and looked back. He had seldom seen Michaels get so upset over something that wasn't a card game or target practice.

"In some bogus sci-fi cheesefest maybe," said Michaels, "but Jesus, man! I mean, this is reality, man, and there's no way they are gonna dig up enough rock to make this scheme of theirs work." Michaels began working with his scrubber again.

Only one mechanic? That did seem strange. Most bases had at least five, working on alternating shifts. Acids in the air and more complex toxins in the rain made the equipment breakdown rate in most populated areas very high.

Griffin frowned. "What was it Sarge said about the atmosphere? A combination of chlorine and fluorine—"

"Uh huh," Michaels said. "So you can figure what *that* would do to O-rings and intake valves and every other goddamned thing." He swiped angrily at the tank; Griffin heard a long, wet thud as goop fell off the inside of the veggie machine.

"What about the VR displays they're using?" Michaels continued, putting down his scrubber again. "I've used those cerebral cortex coils before. That is scary shit, man." He stared at Griffin. "The C.O. said the first group out here was the EC 3rd

Airborne."

"Yeah," Griffin said. "I heard that."

"So where are they?" Michaels said.

Griffin was surprised by the note of genuine fear in the man's voice. Michaels claimed to have been nearly everywhere and done almost everything. Near as Griffin could tell, this was close to true. Not much seemed to flap him. Even the Quantum Gate had made him look more interested than alarmed. Almost against his will, he found himself listening to Michaels.

"When I was in Belgium, I don't know," Michaels moved his hands in a gesture of help-lessness. "I could swear the VR was . . . not accurate. I still don't know what the hell I was shooting at. And they give you a drug."

Griffin remembered a lecture from med school, the instructor talking about an experimental VR enhancement drug. He'd said, "Addiction is a very real threat." What else had he said? Weren't there some odd side effects? Then Griffin shook his head sharply.

"Listen to you!" he said. "You sound paranoid. They can't give us drugs unless we know about it. It's in the contract. Don't go off the deep end, Michaels. Yeah, I agree this place is strange, but they're not going to blow off the contract. Not the UN."

Michaels looked at him for a long second. "All

right, fine, whatever. In a couple of days, you'll stop dreaming. Then you'll believe me."

Michaels went back to work. When they finished the outside, they sealed both ends of the machine and opened the cloacal valve, and Michaels pushed the flush buttons. The kitchen filled with the wet, sucky noise of veggie paste disappearing—to where? Griffin didn't want to think about it. When the flushing stopped, they opened up the far end of the processor and crawled inside for an inspection.

Griffin's half was, as he expected, a lot more work to finish. Michaels was long gone by the time he got it done. As he worked inside the stinking, clanging tube of metal, Griffin tried to think about the simulation runs instead of what Michaels had said. He hadn't joined Beatrice to think. But Michael's last comment haunted him. No dreams. A couple of days and you'll stop dreaming.

That, he remembered, was the major side effect of the VR enhancement drugs—cessation of REM sleep.

No dreams.

Chapter Twelve

By the time Griffin was done cleaning the processor, he smelled like one. He made his first trip to the small bathroom off his room and got a profound shock. He couldn't find the scrubber controls so he began punching buttons and twisting knobs at random. Why didn't they mark these things? After being blasted with hot air, watching the toilet appear and disappear, getting doused with an unpleasantly intense antiseptic of some sort, and confronting an absurdly enlarged image of his own nose, a set of holes in the ceiling doused him with water.

He slapped the valve shut, profoundly shocked. Water?

The chemical and biological toxin levels of most water was so high that a shower could kill you if it wasn't run off refined water, and who could justify washing with the stuff of life itself? Water showers were illegal in most countries, though he had heard that forking over major money could cause apparently disabled fixtures in certain old hotels to suddenly become operational.

He examined the cubicle walls again. There wasn't even an outlet for a sonic cleanser—but there was a grated drain in the floor, and an opening in the ceiling. As he looked at it, a drop of water formed and fell onto his face.

He twisted the knob back on and a steady stream of warm water poured down over his head. He watched in horror as it disappeared into the floor beneath his feet. The potable water situation on AJ3905 must be a lot different than it was on Earth, or they wouldn't have a water shower in an army private's quarters. Still, the thought of using it to clean dirt off his body seemed perverse.

So many people were slowly dying of thirst that the World Health Organization had dreamed up a stupid name for it—CWDS. As if anyone alive didn't know what "Chronic Water Deprivation Syndrome" really meant. Now, he had quantities flowing over his skin that could get a man killed in half the major cities of the world.

How could there be so much safe water on a planet with an atmosphere that could eat your face?

Next to the knob that controlled the water was a tube of soap. He squeezed some out, and he used it to scrub himself. It was very awkward. There must be a trick to getting soap smeared around before the water sluiced it off, but he didn't know what it was. He wound up feeling like a standard brushing unit would have gotten him cleaner. Still, the water flowing over his shoulders and down his back was the most pleasurable thing he had felt in months.

He shut off the shower, watching with slightly sickened satisfaction as the last of the water disappeared into the drain below his feet.

He hit a button he'd found earlier and now knew how to use. The hot air blasts left him dry and only a bit shuddery. He'd have to check around a bit and find out if there was a more standard cleaning device in his bathroom. For now, he was passably clean.

He pulled fresh fatigues from the dispenser and put them on, trying to decide what he wanted to do. The talk with Michaels had left him feeling restless, as though all the suspicions he'd slowly been feeling were taking some shape that he couldn't quite put his finger on, and that he didn't quite trust.

He snapped his fingers. He hadn't seen any of the base's skivvers yet. Maybe he could get into the hangar and check them out. And, while he was there, he could talk to that mechanic and see what was up.

The promise of flying time had been a big plus with this assignment. He wished they had mentioned he would be flying through poison gas, but these days that was pretty close to the situation on

Earth as well. If the air-based simulation runs were accurate, flying here wouldn't feel noticeably different from flying at home, and the number of sudden thermals was far less.

Griffin headed toward the lift. Once again, he saw no one and met no one, and it spooked him. Every military base he'd been on before rang with noise night and day. Right now, he could hear occasional distant booms and clatters, mostly from the mess hall, but no voices. The lift's whine was almost shocking in its volume as he took it down to the first floor. The halls with their overarching struts and energy-woven floors reminded him again of how tough this base was. He had probably never been in a building that could take as many hits as this one could.

The hangar held only two skivvers, both Gamelon Class cruisers that could transport twenty people or be run completely via wire. Beautiful machines. He looked at them a moment, and remembered Saunders talking about the added troops they expected soon. And only two skivvers? Perhaps there were more somewhere else, he thought. Perhaps there was a different base, a second station, on AJ3905—and with that thought a sudden cool relief came over him.

Of course. That had to be it. They were in a start-up station, or perhaps just the entry station and the rest of the operation, the real heart of this expedition, was elsewhere. With miners and skivvers and troops, and hallways that rang with movement and life. They just hadn't mentioned it, that was all.

Griffin smiled and felt his shoulders relax for what seemed like the first time in months, and he turned his attention back to the skivvers. Perhaps there were only two of them, but they were beauties. This was going to be fun. Defused power outriggers were arranged in racks against the far wall, looking like the bombs they potentially were.

The skivver on his right was locked but the main entry hatch of the one on the left irised open as he approached. He climbed aboard. The main hold looked stripped down, with no seats and no cargo latches.

He was impressed. The walls had to be memory enhanced, capable of producing whatever outfitting was needed for a given mission. At the tail end was a set of airlocks and a huge door that looked like it could fit a meta-tank.

The front end had the control cockpit. He climbed into the pilot's chair and ran his hands over the touch-sensitive surfaces. Basic readings answered—air pressure, wind speed, and engine temperature. He smiled as the skivver told him he was standing still and his engine was cold. What else, eh? He gave the warm-up section a tentative tap and nothing happened. Good. Probably passworded.

After he climbed out and stood admiring the sleek beast, he heard a small noise from the far end of the hangar. He walked forward and the door opened in front of him.

A man in a mechanic's uniform and cap bent over a workbench, the lamp above spreading a vee of light over him. A curious clutter of objects filled the shelf behind him. Some were tools, but Griffin couldn't place them as having anything to do with skivvers.

The shelves mostly contained what appeared to be handmade models. A very detailed and lovely old sailing ship, its white sails dusty; an old-style internal combustion truck; a stubby little thing that looked vaguely aerodynamic but had no noticeable means of propulsion; and other objects lost in the shadows.

Griffin walked forward and the mechanic looked up. He appeared to be a bit over forty, with graying hair and a vigorous face. He grinned like Griffin was his best friend.

"Hey, how's it going?" he boomed out. "Name's DiSilva, John DiSilva—how're you doin'?"

"Good," said Griffin, taken aback by the man's enthusiasm.

The mechanic pursed his lips for a moment. "Hey, haven't we met before?"

Griffin peered at him. "Uh, no. I don't think so."

"Oh, sure, sure we have." His voice had a Texas

flavor to it, evoking images of good ol' boys in the dry desert. He waved a gold-toned object that he was holding in his left hand and his brows knitted as he thought. He snapped his fingers and brightened. "On a transport flight into Fort Chicago."

Griffin tilted his head. He'd flown into Fort Chicago just after enlisting, but there were so many people on the plane he couldn't have said anything about those who weren't right next to him. That was only a few days after Jenny's accident. He hadn't been very interested in anything then. The man snapped his fingers again, his face still intent.

"You were going into basic." A volley of finger snaps sounded from his right hand as the man cudgeled his memory. "You were flying from . . . what—" the man snapped his fingers, then grinned brightly. "From California . . . yeah, yeah, right. What's your name?"

"Griffin."

"Right! Good to see you again. How ya been? Hey, come here. Look at this."

The mechanic picked up a glass tube that was about two hand's widths high. It was narrow at the top and belled out toward the bottom. Both ends were capped with metal. He placed it onto the object he had been holding in his left hand, which was obviously its base.

"You know what this is?" he said, looking like a cat with the family canary in its mouth.

Griffin shrugged.

"This is a lava lamp." The mechanic tapped it gently, almost lovingly. "This thing here is almost a hundred years old. It's amazing the stuff they used to do." He smiled at it and shook his head. "This ran on alternating current electricity—at huge voltages." He looked into Griffin's eyes as though he expected him to know what that meant. "There was enough wind running through this thing to kill a man." A sharp nod. "I'm restoring it. Kind of a hobby."

He set it back down on the work bench and lifted the glass part off the base to look at it. "I'm afraid the liquid part congealed a long time ago and I'm not exactly sure what they used, so I'm gonna have to do a little experimenting to figure out what it was. I think," he tapped on the glass, "this is based on glycerin."

"That's, uh, great," Griffin said. "Hey, aren't you kinda taking a chance?"

DiSilva knit his eyebrows. "On what?"

"Well, you know, working on personal stuff while you're on duty."

"Ah, shit no, they don't care." DiSilva burst into laughter. "I got nothing else to do."

"Yeah? Listen, I was sort of wondering—where're the rest of the skivvers?"

The mechanic looked up from the broken lava lamp. "Rest of them?" he echoed. "What do you mean, rest of them?"

"Yeah, there's only two out there, and I thought maybe—"

"No, that's it." DiSilva held up his toy, turning it in the light. "Nice, isn't it?"

"Yeah, yeah it is. Uh, listen, John—maybe they're at the other base?"

DiSilva put the toy down. "The what?"

"The other station. I mean, this is just intake, isn't it? The rest of the skivvers, they'll be at the other station."

"I don't know about that." DiSilva looked down at his toy, then back up at Griffin. "Hey, listen. You better skedaddle. You're not supposed to be back here. Off limits." He looked embarrassed.

Griffin was baffled. Since when was a pilot barred from visiting the hangar? This base was weird.

"But I'm a pilot—"

DiSilva shrugged again, obviously uncomfortable, and wouldn't meet his eyes. "Hey, I don't write 'em, I just follow 'em. You really ought to leave." He glanced up quickly. "I mean, I could get in trouble too, you know."

Griffin decided not to make a point of it, and the mechanic looked relieved as Griffin left the workshop. The door closed behind him.

Michaels was right—this guy clearly had a lot of time for his hobbies. Kind of gave Griffin the creeps. He hadn't been on many bases, but it always seemed to him that mechanics generally had about five times as much work as they could possibly get done. They took their time-outs in deeply hidden corners where no one could find them; not just beyond an unlocked door.

He looked again at the skivver as he walked through the large hangar. Michaels claimed this mechanic was a sign that they were being lied to. But about what? And why? It just didn't make sense.

Ah, never mind that nonsense, he thought with sudden disgust. You didn't join Beatrice International to think, and Michaels could find trouble in a church, and probably had.

Maybe he could log some more simulator time today. The sarge said they should get at least two hours a day, either in real-time missions or simulations. He'd been sick up to here with the simulator when he got out this morning, but now the idea called to him. Kill those bugs. His heart beat faster. Yes.

Chapter Thirteen

The hangar doors irised open, and Griffin headed down the dark and glittering hall. As he rounded the first corner toward the simulation room, he saw two UN people standing in front of the security area talking. They were deeply intent on each other. The blond, Slavic-looking man wore a full-bore UN monkey suit, with a black collar and captain's cummerbund. The dark-haired woman, a guard judging by her uniform, smiled broadly.

"So, what's the problem?" Griffin heard her say as he approached. She tilted her head, looking into the man's eyes flirtatiously.

The man moved his shoulders uncomfortably. "I don't think it would be a good idea."

"Come on, I just asked you over for a drink, what's the problem?"

"Well, I'm an officer, for one thing. . . ."

Her voice turned mocking. "Oh, God, you don't

really. . . ."

The captain saw Griffin approaching and his face darkened.

"Do you need something, solider?" Cold blue eyes calculated him and found him wanting.

Griffin felt his face flush. They both knew he'd overheard the conversation.

"Oh, I'm just leaving."

The guard smiled. She really was a pretty woman. The officer was a fool to hesitate. "No problem," she said and turned away from him.

He backed off, walking hurriedly in the opposite direction of the simulation room. He didn't want any more attention out of UN people than he could avoid. The corridor curved dark ahead of him, lit by golden spots and flanked by red support struts. He heard the guard's light voice say teasingly, "Anyway, I'd like you to come over for a shot of vodka tonight."

"Vodka? Mmm. This has possibilities."

Griffin glanced back as he rounded the corner, and the blond officer was standing much closer to the guard. She smiled brightly into his face. Someone was going to get laid tonight.

The thought suddenly hurt him. He took a few steps more, then stopped in the middle of the corridor. His first time with Jenny. . . .

❖ ❖ ❖

He had been in a hurry that day, intending to meet a couple friends for a show. The Raven Entertainment Mall was right on the outskirts of the Century City enclave, and teemed with people. It claimed to have fully filtered air and light so that you could check your protective gear at the entrance and walk around unencumbered even during toxin alerts. A year later, those claims had been disproved, but who could have forecast such a density of airborne polymers?

That day, it seemed as though everyone in the city was there and all of them were determined to get in Griffin's way. He'd finally made it to a level that wasn't too overrun, but only two of the lifts were working.

He had five minutes to get to the theater, maybe ten if Ruthern was feeling kind. Otherwise, they would go in without him and he'd have to take catch as catch can. These productions were always more fun when you knew at least some of the other actors.

"Excuse me, did you drop this?" said a voice from behind him, and he turned. For a moment, time stopped. She wasn't beautiful, not in any classic way, yet the wildly curling reddish blond hair floating around a triangular face with big eyes held him, spoke to him. She was wearing a low-cut green dress that might have been made of velvet—a daring material to wear these days. Most people avoided cloth that had a nap because it tended to trap allergens and toxins. The dress reminded him vaguely of medieval stories about the maiden who gets saved from the dragon.

"What?" said Griffin, caught between fascination and irritation.

"Did you drop this money?" She held out a bundle of plats. He glanced at it. Looked like a substantial though not flabbergasting amount.

"No." He couldn't figure out why he kept watching her face. She wasn't pretty in the ways that usually caught his attention. Vivid. Yes, that was it. She seemed very vivid.

"Are you sure?" She frowned slightly. "Because I thought I just saw it fall out of your pants pocket." She pointed toward the lifts.

"No, it's not mine. I keep my money in my wallet." He began to turn away.

"You're sure?"

"Yes, I'm sure."

"'Cuz there's a lot of money here." She looked at the wad of plats and shook her head.

"Look—it's not mine," he said. The lady was cute, but her brain must have evaporated with the ozone layer. If he was late, his friends wouldn't wait. Still, she had a nice smile.

She rifled the wad in her hands, then pointed at it. "There's three hundred dollars here."

"Regardless, that is *not* my money!"

"You're sure? 'Cuz this is a lot of money just to

pass up."

"Look—it's not like I'm giving anything up. It was never mine to begin with." Time to go. Past time to go. The lady was just not fully enabled.

"You're telling me you have no claim to this cash?" She patted it, and suddenly grinned at him. What did *that* mean? This had gone on too long. Just walk away. You might make it to the theater in time if you take the stairs and hurry.

"This is correct," he said impatiently. "Yes." He still didn't leave.

She waved the bundle at him. "We could split it."

Griffin raised his hands into the air. "No, I don't want to split that money with you. I don't want a single plat's worth of that money. I don't know who it belongs to and I *don't care*."

She was half-flinching before his vehemence, which made him feel simultaneously guilty and more vehement.

"You may keep it or give it to someone. Hell, you can burn it for all I care."

"Well, all right. I get the point."

She started to turn away. Long curling hair trailed down her back. He had an urge to reach out, tangle his fingers in the mass of it. He turned toward the lifts to see if any were going to arrive soon. He tried to be relieved that the crazy lady was finally going to leave him alone. He stared unseeing at the read-out panel, still thinking about her hair. Wanting to touch it. Wondering how it smelled.

She spoke to him again. He jumped, as embarrassed as if she had caught him actually trying to touch her without permission. She grinned, her face turning triangular. "Um, oh god, y'know what? I'm so embarrassed. I just remembered. This money did not fall out of your pants pocket. It's my money."

You just *remembered* it's your money? Now, wait a minute . . . he started to speak and found all words beyond him. He just gaped at her.

Her smile became more tentative. "I came over here and dropped it because I thought you had a really great ass and I really wanted to meet you."

He was dumbstruck. You thought I had a great ass. You're using a bundle of cash to pick up a guy in a public walkway.

"Can I buy you a latte?" she said, waving the wad. "I've just come into a little cash and I'm feeling generous."

He told himself to walk away. Instead, he nodded. She grinned with delight, skipped forward, and wrapped herself around his right arm. She half-dragged him in the opposite direction of the theater. Ruthern, Sala, and Bend wouldn't care that much if he didn't show up. He'd just tell them he got struck by a tornado.

Griffin didn't like lattes, but he drank three cups that evening. And then they went to a bar and he drank single-malt scotch for the first time. He liked that better.

He was one very wired drunk the first time he'd gone to bed with Jenny. He never quite knew why he'd done it. It wasn't that unusual for women to try to pick him up. But Jenny wasn't usual. She never was. She never would be. She reached for his mind and his heart even before she reached for his body, and he could not have pulled back. Never wanted to pull back. Until later.

Griffin's face was wet with tears. He looked around sharply, afraid he might not have heard someone walking toward him. He wiped his face on his uniform sleeve. What was wrong with him? He'd been able to hold away such thoughts for months. What good was it to think of Jenny? That was all over now. Even if she would be willing to see him again, what could he be for her? She was better off without him. He was better off here.

He felt sick again, as sick as he'd felt this morning, but this time his mind just wouldn't turn off, wouldn't stop the replay of memories. He looked around wildly, seeking anything to distract him, and found a door labeled "Quantum Gate." Without pausing to think, he strode toward it, half expecting a security denial. Instead, the door irised open and let him in.

Chapter Fourteen

A slightly smaller version of the Quantum Gate Griffin had entered in the Fort Chicago hangar occupied the center of the room. The sight made his head feel strange. He looked away, and saw a short man in a yellow uniform looking up at a large display of shifting red and black. The symbol on his back was three overlapping ovals. Griffin frowned. What did *that* mean? He couldn't recall having seen it in the station's heraldry descriptions.

Griffin coughed to announce his presence. The man turned, and his large thick glasses flashed red for a moment from the display. The poor guy must not react well to corrective surgery. Some people didn't and then they had to wear those things on their faces. The tag on his left breast said "Charlie Becker," followed by a bunch of initials and the insignia of ovals again. Griffin couldn't make sense out of any of it.

The little man gave a pinched half smile that looked more like a grimace, "Sorry, guy. This is off limits. You're not allowed back here."

"I didn't realize," Griffin said, "What is this? Is that the Gate?"

"Yeah, sure is," Charlie Becker said, and made no move to toss Griffin out.

Griffin looked around the room uneasily, trying to find something that looked familiar. "Y'know, I don't remember coming through here."

"Most people don't. We don't know why. Dr. Marks thinks it's a product of the profound frequency shift. She thinks it proves that all thought, or at least all memory, is frequency based."

"So, what's the profound frequency shift?"

"Oh, it's Elizabeth's," the man paused over the name, seeming to savor it. "It's *her* theory. It's part quantum mechanics and part," the man lowered his voice in a mocking way, "transcendental vision. Woo-ee!" He raised his hands like a kid saying Boo! "It's the perfect synthesis of intellect," he held up his right hand and made an eating gesture, "and intuition." Then he raised his left hand and brought the two together.

Griffin smiled and nodded as though he understood.

The odd man continued. "She is one of the greatest minds of our age. I'll tell you that right now."

He stared over Griffin's right shoulder. "I am so in love with her."

No, Griffin thought, no, I don't want to know, I don't want to think about—

"Gosh, I have this recurring daydream where I . . . Where I turn around and . . ." He flushed. "Anyway—" he laughed shrilly and gestured toward the display screen. "This is really amazing. It's so simple. It really shouldn't work at all."

Becker turned to look at the screens. Griffin stared at him, feeling cold inside and, quite suddenly, every other emotion disappeared.

"Shouldn't work at all?" he echoed. "The Gate shouldn't work?"

"Oh, I understand completely all the physical processes the Gate uses but uh, I don't quite see how it works." He shrugged violently. "It shouldn't. I don't see how it could take us anywhere. It's almost as if the combination or rather the physical placement of the parts causes a quantum anomaly that allows . . ." and his hands moved in a rolling forward gesture, "the Gate to work. I don't know. Huh. I just don't really see how it works. Elizabeth sees it clearly. Sometimes I wonder . . . I wonder if we really are on AJ3905."

"Where the hell else would we be?" Prickles of fear ran down his spine, and Griffin clenched his fists angrily. He kept looking for answers and getting more questions.

"How would we know?" The little man shrugged again. "We could be in Trinidad. They could have told us we were going to some random number and then just shipped us off to Sumatra!"

He smiled as though this was a delightful idea. Probably was. Griffin imagined the guy fantasizing about Marks and Sumatra and steamy jungles, and pushed the image away.

Becker's face turned serious. "I wonder about that sometimes. I wonder about where we might really be."

"Yeah?" Griffin took a deep breath. "If we're on Earth, then why are we shooting at the natives, Charlie? I mean, are we at war with Sumatra?"

Charlie Becker giggled. "Sumatra? War? Oh, hardly."

"But you said you didn't understand why the Gate works, didn't you? And that we could be somewhere on Earth?"

"Oh, well, really, I don't quite, I mean—" Then Becker focused on something behind Griffin. His face lit up and he beckoned wildly.

"I told him to go," Becker said. "This is restricted, I told him so."

Griffin turned. The UN captain he'd seen earlier out in the hall stepped from beside the door to stand in front of Griffin. By the expression on the blond man's face, Griffin knew he was in trouble. He sighed. Had the man followed him here? Great to have made an officer into an enemy so soon.

"What are you doing?" said the UN man. "I told you, you're not supposed to be here."

The officer whipped out a small electronic camera, flashed it at Griffin, and examined the readout.

"Private Griffin, you're now on report." He stepped aside and gestured toward the door.

On report? Oh great. What a jerk! Griffin bit down a half-dozen possible replies. Such as, the officer had given him a move-along in the corridor but had *not* told him he couldn't go into the lab. He knew this guy's type—anything he said would just make things worse. He stared at the captain for a moment. Becker peered anxiously over the captain's shoulder. Griffin nodded coldly and walked out.

Chapter Fifteen

The simulators were nearby now, but the idea of another run didn't seem appealing anymore. He wanted to be alone in a quiet place. The thought of going back to his room gave him the shudders. Where could he go to just sit?

The atrium! There had to be an entrance to it on this floor. He'd seen a couple of benches dotted about but only once seen someone sitting on one.

The entrance to the atrium wasn't marked on the maps, but he wandered around on the first floor until he found it opposite the airlock. The sweet moist smell of growing plants filled his nostrils as the door irised open.

Someone was already there, standing near the statue and looking up at the light pouring down. He hesitated, thought about turning around, then realized it was Marie Lukas, the nurse from sick bay.

"Hey!" she said, and her broad face creased in

a smile.

He returned her smile, genuinely pleased to see her. She seemed so solid, so human. She had an air about her that made him think she never got confused about reality or responsibility. She knew what was what and held to it.

"Do you believe this?" Marie said and gestured up.

His gaze followed her hand past twining lengths of leafy green and several layers of doors and vents. At the apex of the atrium was a circle of glowing glass. Traces of blue and white refracted in the glass. He looked back at her.

"Uh, what's that?"

"The dome." He looked up again and she continued. "It looks just like a sky. I can't believe it."

She shook her head. Then she smiled, and posed herself to look coy. "I'm out here working on my tan." They both laughed. She had about as deep a natural tan as anyone was likely to get.

"I wonder how it's done?" said Griffin.

Marie frowned. "I don't know. I thought it was that Spectrastone stuff, like the walls, but it looks too good for that, too real, doesn't it? I mean, look at this—this is *real* sunlight." She waved her hands at the light streaming down. "I can't figure out for the life of me why they went to all this trouble. Not that I'm complaining! You know, supposedly it duplicates the sky on Earth from five hundred years ago and it's matched with the time on Earth. So, when it's five o'clock back home, it's five o'clock here."

"So, which city is it matched to?"

"Well, you know, that's a good question. Probably New York. You know how the UN is." She shrugged. "But you gotta figure they get it right." She laughed suddenly. "Either that, or they fake it real good. Like this flowers stuff—I'm a city girl, I know what grass looks like and that's about it. But this stuff, for all I know it could be made up in some lab somewhere."

Griffin looked at the plants, then looked at Marie Lukas again.

"Do you think it is?" he said.

She shrugged and stood. "I don't know, soldier boy. Tell you one thing, though. This city girl's gonna be real happy to get back to Earth, you know what I mean? It may not be any great shakes anymore, but it's home." She looked around unhappily. "And this place sure ain't."

She nodded to him and walked down the path toward the door. Griffin sat on the nearest bench, watching that lovely bright light. It'd been nice to chat but it was nicer still just to feel the warmth, the heavy sweetness of the air, and the slightly damp bench underneath him. Idly, he fingered a small, lilylike flower that leaned over the bench. It was bright orange shading to yellow, with brown spots at its heart, clustered with others at the end of a curving stem.

It fell off of its stem and rested in his palm. He snapped his fingers shut around it, expecting an AP to show up to chide him, or that uptight UN captain to march in and put him on report again. When nothing happened, he slowly opened his fingers again and looked.

It was beautiful, an intricate but smooth flaring of petals and stamen. He sniffed it, enjoying the lovely scent. Then, very carefully, he put it and his hand in his pocket, and returned to his room.

He found a glass in the bathroom and cautiously poured an inch of water into it, then floated the tiny flower in the water. Its sweet smell filled the room.

"Dinner will be ready in the mess hall in ten minutes. Please report to the mess hall for dinner in ten minutes."

Griffin automatically tucked the impromptu vase behind him, but it was only the AP, whose pretty face gazed out at him from the Militerm screen. Griffin frowned at it for a moment, wondering if his room was being monitored. He'd never really worried about having his billet surveyed before—privacy was a right you specifically signed away when you joined Beatrice—but he didn't feel right about the flower, and didn't want to get rid of it, either. Finally he hid it against the wall, behind the pile of his books, and headed out for dinner.

Hynick and Castle were already waiting for the mess hall AP to serve them when he arrived. Hynick, ever hopeful, was trying out his wiles again. The boy astonished Griffin. Castle, tough and mature and sarcastic, was even less likely to fall for Hynick than Dr. Mirren.

Dinner was even worse than lunch. How *did* they do it? Macaroni and cheese just wasn't a complex meal. The noodles were amazingly tough, which he'd expected, but the cheese sauce was truly amazing. He hadn't realized that you could get melted plastic to smell that way.

Alonzo and Tisch came in as he was arranging the macaroni into lines of soldiers on his plate. He waved them over for the distraction. He had to eat this stuff but he didn't have to think about it.

"How you doing?" Griffin asked as he took another bite.

"I've been better." Tisch put down his tray. "Did the doc say anything about how long this Gate lag stuff lasts?"

Alonzo pulled up a chair. "A day or two is what I hear."

"Great," said Tisch and ate a forkful of the indecently orange food. His face folded into a grimace. "Let's say we entertain ourselves in the meantime by hanging the cook."

"Then we'd get to eat your cooking?" said Alonzo. "No way. I've survived worse than this."

Griffin gave him a skeptical glance and then went back to his food. Alonzo had always seen worse, eaten worse, and done worse than anyone else. Only Michaels bothered with trying to compete.

"What do you think of our new C.O.?" said Griffin.

"Tough as nails and twice as ambitious." Tisch nodded tightly for emphasis.

Griffin raised an eyebrow. "What's new? Aren't they all?"

"You talked with anyone on this base yet?" Tisch asked.

"Naw," Griffin said. "Just a nut mechanic and a really strange little guy who works on the Quantum Gate."

"Charlie Becker? Yeah, he's a piece of work," Alonzo said. "He hangs out in the enlisted lounge, writing wildly in his journal."

"Great," Griffin said. "With our luck, he'll be in charge of entertainment at tonight's reception. Or that mechanic, with his toys."

"No," Tisch said. "I mean some of the UN folks. Have you talked to any of them?"

"I got put on report by a blond jerk with a stick up his ass."

Tisch laughed. "Captain Zhorchow. Yeah, a righteous dude, that one. Well, I caught up with a guard and she says Saunders has *very* big plans. He's a fast-track guy and he's acting like he's found the stairway to heaven. He's been keeping Dr. Marks on a short leash, and they don't think it is just 'cuz she's got a good bod. I suppose saving the world would be worth a promotion or two, but if that's the case, why don't we have a general in charge? There's something funny going on around here."

"OK, so Saunders has a lot of pull and got himself a plum assignment," said Alonzo. "And since when isn't there something funny going on? We're in an army, guys, in case you hadn't noticed. The whole thing is a laugh riot. Have you noticed our rifles all have a child-proof orange safety ring?"

"Get off!" said Griffin.

"No lie. Look it up in Militerm if you don't believe me."

"Child proof, eh? Does that mean Hynick is released from duty?" They looked over to where Castle was grinning tolerantly at the red-faced boy. Tisch laughed so hard tears streamed down his face.

Chapter Sixteen

Back in his room, Griffin casually wandered over to his small stack of books as if to check the titles. The flower was still hidden behind them, floating in the glass like a small piece of beauty in this dark, sinister place. He touched it with a fingertip, sending it skimming the surface of the water to butt gently against the far side of the glass.

He changed into his dress uniform, signaled the door into mirror mode, and checked himself. The red Beatrice patch on the back of his dress greens made him feel like a target, but at least the inside didn't itch anymore. Whoever picked the thread for the embroidery must have gotten hot off imagining people in pain. Hawkins had clued him to a tailor who would line it with felt.

He heard voices in the entryway and decided he was as beautiful as he was going to get. Time to head down to the reception.

Whalen, Hawkins, and Alonzo looked up as his door opened. Hawkins smiled, Alonzo nodded, and Whalen looked nervous. They were all wondering how tonight would go. He had heard that the first reception on a new base was always strange. It could get wild after the C.O. left. It could get boring. It could, in many ways, shape the feeling of their time at the station—nobody took it casually.

By common consent, they decided not to wait for the rest of the platoon. It was nearly nineteen-hundred, and better to be on time than all together. They moved in a clump toward the lift.

Whalen pressed her nose to the glass of the lift as it descended and tried to identify the plants.

"Oh, who cares what they are? It's pretty, isn't it?" said Alonzo.

"You don't understand. I don't know formal botany, but my mother always had an enclosed garden going and I used to help her a lot. The garden was pretty important to us for food. She really knows her plants and there just aren't that many different kinds, not among those in common use."

Griffin kept his mouth shut. Under other circumstances he would have joined the conversation, not even caring whether the lift was bugged or not, but this time it just didn't feel right.

"So, maybe these are uncommon plants, eh?" Alonzo suggested.

"It's so strange. They all look roughly familiar but none of them are quite right when I look at the details. Like, that tree's a maple but what type? I don't get it." When the doors opened on the first door, she hung back, still looking at the atrium with a puzzled expression on her face.

"Don't sweat it," said Hawkins gently. "There must be someone around here who knows. Ask around at the reception."

Whalen nodded, and followed them reluctantly, looking back once as the door closed against the bright light of the atrium.

They walked down the quiet hall into the main corridor. The Gate was running again, its hum perceived more as a vibration in the deck than as a noise. Alonzo glared toward it as they turned right toward the briefing and simulation room, where the reception was taking place. To Griffin's astonishment, the big man crossed himself. Griffin himself was a lukewarm theist, having adopted the Gaia faith his mother espoused, but he'd never seen someone do the sign of the cross outside a movie.

Griffin turned his eyes away, a little embarrassed to have seen it, and instead watched Whalen's strong and narrow back as she walked toward the briefing room. He'd gone to bed with her once. Most of the platoon had tried each other out that way. It had been nice but not exactly hot for either of them. She had talked about her family and he had thought about Jenny. Yet, that was the way sex within the platoon mostly worked.

Michaels thought the company used conditioning to keep it that way. If so, it probably wasn't a bad idea. On some assignments, quarters could get very close. A little sex was fine, but if it got into love, things could get really bad really fast. Witness how fast he and Jenny—no, this wasn't the right time to think about that.

Why was he having so much trouble staying away from these thoughts? It was like something in his brain was picking at him to torture himself.

As they rounded the curving corridor, they saw Tisch, Michaels, and Sarge standing in the hall outside the briefing room, waiting for things to get started.

"Sure hope the food here is better than in the mess hall," said Michaels.

"Why would it be? All comes from the same place." Hawkins didn't look at Michaels, and his expression was uncharacteristically impatient.

"Yeah. Griffie and I just spent most of the afternoon cleaning it, too." Michaels held his nose. "You don't want to know, you really don't."

"Maybe Cookie will take special pains for tonight," said Whalen.

"Maybe Cookie will get stage fright and leave it all up to his mess hall AP. Betcha that'd be an improvement."

Sarge cleared her throat, and their heads whipped around. The colonel strode past them, closely followed by a very tight-faced Dr. Marks. As the door closed behind them, the platoon exchanged glances uneasily. The tension between Saunders and Marks was like a solid fog. Something was going on, and the platoon members half-wanted to speculate, but were afraid of being overheard.

Sarge started talking about the day's simulation runs, accusing them all of being scared to shoot bugs. She got a chorus of amused outrage. As Griffin joined in the hooting, he wondered if the others felt the same way he did. He was getting flashes of near-idiot joy at the thought of killing bugs, as though there was nothing in the world that could make him happier. Felt sorta creepy. Yet how else could you feel about things that were so ugly and so violent?

Cookie opened the doors. Saunders, Marks, her assistant Dr. Li, Andrews, and several UN officers stood in a loose line near the door, not quite a formal greeting party but pretty close. Griffin was introduced to Captain Zhorchow. He shook the man's hand and received another cold glare in return. Great, just great. That guy must practice in a mirror every morning before starting his day, making sure he looked nasty enough.

The food was prettier than in the mess hall, but no tastier. Hynick, John DiSilva, and Alvarez arrived in a clump while Griffin was testing a cheese ball. The hangar mechanic's booming voice filled the room, making it almost seem like a party. Griffin had moved on to the so-called ham when Dr. Mirren and her nurse, Marie Lukas, came in.

Dr. Mirren caused a wave of silence through the room. She was not wearing a standard dress uniform. At least, Griffin had never seen one cut that low with a shiny flowing skirt. Hynick about dropped his teeth, but Griffin noticed he also rubbed his butt surreptitiously and made no effort to get close. Nearly every man and half the women in the room started an automatic drift toward the spectacular doc.

Dr. Marks and the colonel barely glanced at each other and kept a stiff minimum distance of half a meter, but were almost never farther from each other than that. No one stood between them, even when there was room—it would probably feel like grabbing two hot wires to stand in the path.

The pretty UN guard Griffin had seen earlier walked in. Michaels glanced at her and put down his plate.

"Griffie, kid, I'm going to be a busy man," he said, grinning.

Griffin rolled his eyes. "You are a piece of work, Michaels. You're gonna put the make on the UN?"

Michaels' grin didn't change, but it didn't reach his eyes, either. "If that's what it takes, sure, I don't mind boinking the lady. Jeez, kid, get a grip. I'm going to find out what in hell's going on around here."

Griffin looked at the guard dubiously. "First of all, I saw her putting her own make on Zhorchow the Stick—the uptight UN captain over there. And second, what makes you think she knows any more than we do?"

"My son," Michaels replied, "when the package looks like that, it never hurts to try."

A minute later, Michaels and the guard were exchanging quiet words. Captain Zhorchow looked furious and jealous. Griffin was tempted to tell Zhorchow that ladies usually dumped Michaels fairly fast, but he didn't figure it would improve the man's mood. Besides, maybe the guard was paying him back for not acting interested until she'd offered him vodka.

He heard Hawkins say, "Does anyone know if they have a language?"

Griffin turned and was in a circle of five people, several of whom he'd never seen before.

"Who cares? All they do is rip at us and we have to fight back." The speaker was a UN man.

"We're on their turf, aren't we?" said Hawkins. "Why shouldn't they blast at us? The colonel says they are intelligent. If we could talk to them, maybe we could get them to help with the mining."

The UN man's face said he thought that Hawkins

was pitifully naive. "Don't you think Saunders would have thought of that? He's got a civilian lab here and they're studying everything about this planet. Do you think we're fighting them just for fun? We all know it would be cheaper to mine if we could use indigenous labor. But do those critters look like something that might pick up a shovel and follow orders?"

An assenting silence swept the group, and even Hawkins looked doubtful. No, they sure didn't. You couldn't tell everything from appearance, though—Jenny had thought he looked like a good man.

Griffin veered away from that thought, and remembered what Michaels had said that afternoon: "I could swear the VR was . . . not accurate." Not accurate. Did the UN even know for certain what the bugs looked like?

Chapter Seventeen

Saunders and Marks were finally speaking but still looked unhappy. Saunders had a hand on the doctor's left wrist and was moving his thumb over the back of her hand while talking urgently in low tones. Marks pulled at her hand, not quite yanking it away but clearly not pleased with the man's grip. She said something quiet and, by the expression on her face, very bitter.

"Interesting pair, aren't they?" said Dr. Mirren. He hadn't noticed her come up to stand beside him.

"Who do you mean?"

"Don't be coy. Marks and Saunders."

Griffin glanced back at the couple. Saunders looked confused and a little hurt, like a child whose toy has been taken away. Did he actually care for Dr. Marks?

"I guess."

She snorted. "I know sex when I see it. Poor Dr. Marks."

Griffin grunted noncommittally.

"You wonder why I say that, don't you?"

Griffin shrugged and sipped at his glass of synthetic scotch.

"Marks always wins. That's her life. She's so smart it's scary but she's so used to having things go her way she can barely deal with a hangnail. Saunders knows why he went after her, and he's willing to keep the deal he offered. She's only just starting to figure out that it isn't just her sterling qualities. It's sour in her stomach."

"What deal did he offer?"

Dr. Mirren gave him an opaque look, and he felt like he had just flunked some kind of test.

Saunders said something else. Marks's face went white and she jerked her hand away. She put her drink down on the table with a clunk, and spoke briefly to Dr. Li. They both left the room without saying good-bye to anyone. The C.O.'s face twisted briefly as he watched her go out the door. Then his expression smoothed back into a cold mask.

Suddenly, Griffin knew what the deal was. Saunders wanted something from Marks, but had genuinely fallen in love with her. Unwilling, unhappy, real-time love. Griffin looked back at Dr. Mirren, started to speak, and stopped. She grinned and nodded.

She tossed off the rest of her glass, and looked around the room. Several people looked back, hoping to catch her eye.

"Think I should tag Hynick?" she said.

Griffin gaped, startled by the change of topic, then laughed.

"Depends on what you want. He rubs his ass every time he lays eyes on you."

"Yep. But sometimes it is good to show a boy what's what before letting him get away with anything."

"If you say so."

Her gaze was focusing on the skinny private. He looked back, obviously a bit alarmed, and obviously more than a bit entranced. Griffin didn't think Mirren saw the boy as anything but a set of hormone levels. Well, that was how Hynick saw Dr. Mirren, so maybe it was a fair match. Without looking back at him, Dr. Mirren started walking toward Hynick.

Griffin shook his head and took another sip of his drink. The intense smoky fluid warmed his throat. It wasn't a bad rendition of a single malt. He wondered which one it was supposed to be. Glenmorangie?

Michaels was still talking with the pretty UN guard, leaning over her. She smiled up at him, but Griffin saw her glance casually around Michaels arm, making sure that Zhorchow was watching. He was.

"That Michaels, he has all the luck."

Griffin turned to see Lopez standing next to him,

looking angry and more than a little drunk.

"I don't know. I think she's going to dump him for the blond guy."

Lopez just shrugged. "Not what I meant, man. You seen Michaels and the sarge?"

Griffin kept his jaw from dropping. "The *sarge*?"

"Yeah, no shit. I saw him come out of her billet this afternoon."

Griffin shrugged. "So? Maybe she was just chewing him out."

"Yeah? If she was, he was sure enjoying it. Had that same look on his face as after that girl at Port Chicago, remember?"

Griffin, reluctantly, remembered. "Drop it, Lopez. It's none of our business. I mean it. Besides, seems to me like Hynick's the lucky one tonight."

"Hah!" said Lopez, and drained his glass. "That's not luck, that's child molestation."

Griffin laughed. "Yeah, the doc knows what she's about and I doubt he does. Well, he's above the age of consent and I wouldn't mind consenting to that lady."

"Or Dr. Marks, for that matter."

"You think so? She seems pretty severe to me."

"Protective shielding. Some of the softest and sweetest ladies are tough as nails on the outside."

"If you say so."

Lopez nodded ferociously, as though he had just won an argument, and headed for the bar. Griffin watched, thinking about how soft Jenny was from the outside and how tough she was at heart.

The room seemed to recede, fading away as reality had faded away so often recently. He fought it and then, leaning into a corner, just let it take him, no longer bothering to fight.

Their last fight had been over her desire to have children. They'd been living together for nearly two years, she was near the end of her internship, and she thought it was the right time. She wanted to apply for a license to rear children together.

He had figured she was joking the first time she mentioned it, or maybe just spinning a pleasant fantasy. Their life together wasn't perfect, but he was happy and he knew that she was also, most of the time. Why should they make such a big change? Why now? In a few more years, he would be done with his training, they could get established in their practices, build up a little money. . . .

"And then what? I'll be thirty-five and my odds of getting infections or other complications will be rising all the time. What if it takes us a while to get pregnant? A year, two years. Pretty soon we'd be pushing the age limit. After forty, no SWA coverage for me. The economy just can't afford the complication rates of older births."

"There are no risk factors in either of our families. Why are you so worried?"

"I'm not worried. I'm telling you why it is stupid to wait. My body is at the prime age for doing this."

"Your body certainly is prime." He reached for her and she batted his hands away.

"Don't pull that on me now. I'm talking about our future here."

"No, you aren't. You're talking about the future that *you* want to force onto me." His voice turned sharp even as his heart fell. They were going over the same path again.

But that time hadn't followed the same path as before. She was deeply serious about her wish for a child and infuriated at him for refusing to get his shunt reversed. They said terrible things to each other that night. He sneered at her for wanting to bring a child into this messed-up world. She told him she would find someone else who was willing to be a father. He told her he wouldn't raise someone else's kid just because she was letting herself be jerked around by her hormones. She screamed at him that he didn't want a child because he still was one.

That last one hurt the most. It was too close to his fears. What if she died in childbirth? Women did, more all the time. What if she didn't die but focused completely on the baby? He would no longer be real to her. Would no longer be real to himself.

So he had driven her out, hurt and enraged her with sarcasm and contempt, let her storm out of the house and drive away alone.

And she had never come back.

"I'll pay you a penny not to tell me what you're thinking." The sick bay nurse was standing in front of him, looking into his face with gruff concern.

Griffin tried to smile, and saw by her face he hadn't done a good job of it. "I'm not feeling so good. Gate lag, I guess. I'd best head out."

"Probably so. You check in with us again if you keep on feeling lousy."

"So you can get out your horse needle?"

She grinned, black eyes sparkling in her broad face. "It's not a horse needle. They're smaller."

"I'll bet!"

Hynick and Dr. Mirren were already gone. Captain Zhorchow and the guard stood close to each other in a corner; she lifted her face to him, laughing. Griffin looked around the room and finally saw Michaels and the sarge, standing together with a few other members of the platoon. Michaels and the sarge. He didn't want to think about it.

He looked for Saunders, and didn't see him. Usually the C.O. made a big deal of leaving a party, so folks would know they could start letting their hair down. Not this time, he guessed, or he had just missed it. So, there was no one left he had to take leave of by protocol. Griffin walked.

Chapter Eighteen

Whalen caught up with him in the corridor and touched his shoulder. They walked into the lift atrium together and stood for a moment, looking into the dense foliage. The overhead light was off now.

Griffin pointed up. "I was talking to Marie Lukas, the nurse, earlier," he said. "She told me the lights were keyed to Earth's—probably to New York time."

"So it's nighttime in New York," Whalen said. She yawned. "God, I could use a good night's sleep. I feel like I haven't slept in days, even though I have." She yawned again. "Gate lag?"

Griffin took a deep breath.

"No," he said. "I don't think so. I wasn't sleeping well for three or four days before we came through."

Whalen didn't say anything as Griffin took her hand and steered her back into the corridor. They walked silently until they reached the airlock and

Griffin gestured, turning them both to enter the atrium hallway again, and then into the atrium itself. The spiral of lights was still on and cast a dim, almost moonlit, glow over the plants. Instead of sitting on the bench, they stood within a screen of foliage, and Whalen put her hand out to touch a leaf.

"Beautiful," she breathed. "But I swear to God, Griffin, I thought I knew the trees. . . ."

"Yeah," he replied quietly. "I know. It's just one more strange thing."

"Like not dreaming?" she said. "Michaels was muttering about that. And how this station seems deserted, and why Militerm won't cough up any area maps—shit, we're supposed to fight out there, the least they could do is give us some idea of the terrain."

Griffin nodded. "Listen, I've got a theory, though. What if this isn't the only station on AJ3905? That would explain a lot, wouldn't it?"

The pale oval of Whalen's face looked at him, indistinct in the dimness. "Yeah?"

"Yeah. Listen, if there was another station, that would be where the miners are. And the rest of the equipment—you know there are only two skivvers here? So unless someone's taken the rest of them out for a spin, or has them hidden somewhere—" He shook his head. "There's got to be another station, Whalen. It's the only answer."

She was silent for a moment, and Griffin took a deep breath, inhaling the scent of growing plants and damp earth and the small, elusive sweetness of the lilylike plant by the bench.

"Maybe," she said finally. "But what about the dreams, Griffin? And what about this?" She touched a frond above her head. "Listen, it's more than just knowing my mother's plants. I know some botany, it's kinda like a hobby. It's something I want to do, when my enlistment's up. And I swear, this isn't anything like anything I've ever known before."

Her fingers turned the frond gently, pale in the dimness against the darkness of the plant. "You ever had something give you the creeps, Griffin? Well, this gives me the creeps." She looked up at him. "I don't know where we are. I don't know what's out there. I don't trust the C.O., and I think I don't trust Cranshaw any more, either. If there was another station, Griffin, they'd have told us about it. No reason not to. If there really are bugs out there, and we've got to fight them, why not let us see the terrain, get some idea of where we are?"

She stared at him for a moment, and he stared back. Then, silently, she turned and left him in the darkness of the atrium.

Chapter Nineteen

Griffin shed his dress greens with a sigh of relief. The stiff fabric chafed his skin. He stepped into the bathroom, twisted the knob for a short shower, and tried not to flinch as water poured over him. What a day.

He cycled the shower to hot air, pulled a robe from the dispenser, and walked out into his room. The bed looked inviting but he wasn't quite ready for sleep. He went over to the pile of books and picked out his journal, but instead of reading it, he looked down at the flower.

It seemed to move by itself, then the daydreams took him again, except that this time he saw his room, saw the bunk and the terminal and the chair, and at the same time he was inside an old oil painting. Adam and Eve faced the serpent coiling around the tree as it tempted them. Griffin wanted to warn them about knowledge, how the apple could kill them, but he could not speak. Beyond the naked figures was Jenny, her sweet face smiling from behind the trees. He tried to go to her. She changed into Dr. Marks, who said with her voice shaking, "The future of our race is at stake here." The sky darkened and a huge spiderlike bug crossed in front of him. He backed away, filled with intense fear and yet finding it intensely beautiful. Even inside his dream, he wondered how a bug could remind him of Jenny.

Cranshaw said, "Exposure to the atmosphere of AJ3905 is very hazardous." Saunders said, "All aspects of this operation are being governed by the International Indentured Forces Act." Jenny blew him a kiss. He reached for her. Michaels grabbed his arm and said, "They give you a drug. A couple days, you'll stop dreaming. A couple days, you'll stop dreaming. They give you a drug. Stop dreaming." And Whalen tilted a face toward him that was only a pale, blank oval and said, "It gives me the creeps, Griffin. It gives me the creeps."

"Time for lights out. Lights out, Phoenix Company. I hope you all get a good night's sleep."

Griffin jerked out of it, to find himself still standing beside the bookshelf. The journal had slipped out of his hands, and as he bent to pick it up a wave of dizziness overcame him. He dropped the journal onto the shelf and staggered toward his bed.

"Lights out, Phoenix Company," the AP said

again. "I hope you all get a good night's sleep."

He twisted the blankets into a tangled nest and tried to bury himself away from all the worries, and the questions, and the endless, endless lies.

Chapter Twenty

"Good morning, Private Griffin. Please wake up."

Griffin moaned and put his arm across his face. He felt as though he hadn't slept in days and his body ached—the lights in his billet seemed grotesquely bright.

"Wake up, Private Griffin."

The voice, he knew from experience, would continue its even, friendly, unbendable demand until his body left the bunk. Then it would start nagging him to report to the mess hall for breakfast. He swung his legs over the edge of the bunk and sat for a moment.

Malfunctioning VRs, mysterious water, unknown drugs, crazy techs—he shook his head, trying to clear it. Had he really believed all those things yesterday? This was a strange mission, for sure, but the rest was too ridiculous for words. He washed and brushed, pulled a fresh uniform from the dispenser, and headed for the mess hall.

The AP for the food dispenser was still ridiculously cute. She wore a white cap and low-cut waitress outfit. Griffin wondered idly if Private Whalen saw the AP as a sexy young guy.

"Hi! Welcome to the mess hall! The twenty-four-hour special is," the AP paused and gave him a big smile, "PB and J with the crusts cut off!"

He punched for the sandwich tiredly. Sheesh. It made cutting the crusts off sound like the next best thing to sex. A wafflish sort of tray slid out, bearing a glass of orange juice and a white plate with a white sandwich. He took it to the nearest table, sat down, and reluctantly picked up the sandwich. It felt stale. He took a bite.

Amazing. It was like grape-flavored sawdust. He glared at the offending sandwich as he chewed. Michaels claimed it wasn't coincidence that army food tasted terrible. "Hey, man—they want to keep us in fighting trim. They make that stuff on the spot, right down to the molecules. So they can make it taste any way they want. They don't want us to like it too much. Food's expensive and who wants fat grunts?"

A voice sounded above him, "Hey!" Griffin looked up. It was Cookie. He smiled and said, "How's the food?"

"Uh, it's OK." Griffin really didn't want to talk

to that kook any more than he had to. KP duty this afternoon again.

Cookie looked positively hurt. "Waddya mean, it's OK? I programmed that recipe myself. I *know* what I'm doing. I used to be on television! Let me taste that."

The cook plucked the sandwich right out of his hand. Griffin was so flabbergasted he didn't even object. The man took a bite.

"Damn," said the cook and stuck his tongue out several times as though trying to air wash it. "I see your point." He set Griffin's sandwich down and walked away.

Griffin looked at the now diminished sandwich. He supposed he was going to eat it, but it certainly hadn't gotten more attractive in the last few minutes.

A shadow fell across his plate and he looked up again. It was Dr. Marks. She smiled. Griffin stared. Too old for me, but that really is one fine-looking woman. Hardly looks like the same person as that hard lady at the briefing yesterday.

She gestured toward the chair opposite him with a hand that was carrying a cup of coffee. "Excuse me, do you mind if I sit here?"

"No. Please. Help yourself." He half rose in old-fashioned manners, but she had already seated herself.

"Hi. I'm Elizabeth."

"Hi. I'm . . . Andrew."

"Griffin. Yes, I know. Don't you go by Drew?"

"How did you know that?"

"I have a good memory for names and faces. I guess I saw it in your service record or something. I don't know." She took a sip of her coffee, then set it down and began stroking her chin nervously. "You were at the briefing yesterday, weren't you?

"Yes, I was."

She shook her head a bit. "I remember thinking what a kind face you have." Her eyes met his and she smiled. "I hope you don't mind my joining you."

"Oh, no, no. No. Not at all."

"I'm rather embarrassed about yesterday. I . . . didn't behave very well, I'm afraid."

"I was wondering about that."

She wound her hands together and looked down at them. "It all suddenly seemed . . . very hopeless." She took another sip of her coffee. "Can I ask you something?"

"Sure."

"Why did you leave medical school?"

"That's a direct question."

"It's a very good thing to be a doctor, Drew."

Griffin sighed, feeling not quite angry but more than a little annoyed. "Nothing personal, but there's a bit of difference between a medical doctor and a plain old Ph.D."

"You're right. But you know what? I'm *both*." She grinned like a kid pulling off a particularly good stunt.

"Whoops! Really?" He felt his face heating up.

"Yes, I was a pediatrician."

"Did you like it?"

"Yes. Very much. Those little round heads, those little hands." Her face filled with longing as her hands played out the shape of an infant. "Yes, I loved it very much."

"So, why did you stop?"

"A little girl died. Someone I got . . . too close to." The doctor hung her head and her shoulders trembled. Griffin was astonished. People who got that upset about losing a patient seldom made it all the way through medical school. The death rate from infections alone was so high these days. True, children were always the worst, especially if you let yourself get attached, but she must have had an amazingly good track record on deaths to have been hit so hard after having been in practice.

Mirren said that Marks was used to winning, that she nearly always did. What must it be like to live that way? Griffin couldn't imagine. He was used to losing.

Dr. Marks' silence stretched so long he began to feel uneasy. "Uh, are you OK?"

She nodded but didn't look up right away. When she did, her face was sad but clear. "I have a family on Earth. A large family. My mum, my dad, my sisters. And my little girl."

"Oh, yeah. Um." I've got a lover, but I abandoned her. "Thank God you're going to have a chance to help them."

"Do you believe in karma?" She didn't seem to have heard him. "Do you believe we pay for our sins?"

All the time, thought Griffin, but she didn't give him a chance to speak.

"We believe that murder is the worst possible crime a man could commit. We've *killed* our mother. Who judges us? If I'm doing the right thing. . . . Maybe death *is* the price for our sins. But can a whole race of people sin? And what about all the babies and the children and—"

Then Charlie Becker hustled up to stand right at her shoulder, almost touching her. He beamed down, ignoring Griffin. He looked ready to drool.

"Hi, Elizabeth," he said and gave her a big smile with a odd little waggle of his fingers. "Do you need somebody to talk to?"

Dr. Marks looked at him sadly but patiently. "No, Charlie. Thank you. That's very kind of you, but I need to get back to the lab."

She looked at Griffin. "Good-bye. Thanks for listening." Then she got up from the table and left, walking slowly.

Charlie said, "That was uncalled for," in an offended tone and drank some of his orange juice. Griffin was tempted to say something about people who butt into other people's conversations, but figured it wasn't worth it.

"Hey, have a seat," he said. Perhaps, this time, he could get Charlie Becker to talk some more about the Quantum Gate, and his speculations about where they were. But the little man just gave him a wild look, almost as if he had been frightened. He scuttled out.

Very strange, Griffin thought, picking up his PB and J—with the crusts cut off. The doctor felt guilty about something. Here she was, running a project that could save the entire Earth, and she spent her time remembering a dead child and talking about payment for sin. And why had she said, "We've killed our mother"? That's how people talked about Gaia, about the Earth's ecosystem. But we're here to rescue Gaia, aren't we? Why is she using the past tense? Doesn't she believe Project Eden will work?

It made the hair stand up on his arms. Michaels says we can't believe what they are telling us. What was Dr. Marks just telling me?

Whalen and Castle came in. Whalen's face was red and swollen. Castle's hard features looked almost motherly as she ushered Whalen to a chair in the corner and then went to the mess hall AP. Whalen turned to face the wall and Griffin could see that she was crying again.

When Castle passed carrying two trays, he waved her over and she came, glancing anxiously at

Whalen.

Griffin pointed at the private. "What's up?"

"Kansas City torched last night. Listen, would you let Hawkins know if you see him? I think Whalen would like to talk with him."

"You bet. Let me know if I can help."

Castle's mouth twitched in a brief flash of her usual sarcasm. Griffin thought about his conversation with Whalen last night—about her mother's kitchen garden. Whalen's folks lived in Kansas City.

Had lived in Kansas City. Oh, dear god.

Castle, seeing his expression, nodded. "Yeah," she said. "Listen, there is something you can do. Whalen's going to take compassionate leave for the rest of the day—can you tell Sarge?"

"Yeah," Griffin said, feeling sick. He thought about how he'd feel if L.A. torched, then felt ashamed of himself for spinning off Whalen's tragedy. He dumped the rest of his meal in the recycler and headed back to his room.

Kansas City dead! Gaia! Everyone had known that experiment in the Gulf was harebrained. Papa Maynard, the Green's main AI, had been shoving out terabytes of criticism ever since the initial proposal to increase atmospheric oxygen by seeding algae. Papa had even forecast the possibility of major fires. However, even Papa hadn't predicted the firestorm.

According to Tisch, who maintained contact with other Green fanatics outside the army, the meteo-

rologists had been going berserk ever since it started, talking about oxygen-rich winds coming off
thousands of acres of wildly growing algae and slow-
moving storm fronts. Everyone else just watched
in horror as a vast roll of fire moved slowly up the
center of the nation, with the earth itself catching
fire in places. The towering columns of smoke were
visible from Moonbase, looking like a dirty thumb
had smudged the green and brown continent.

Griffin stopped suddenly, standing alone in the
curving corridor of the quiet base, remembering his
mother talking about the information she'd picked
up at a Green rally less than a year ago. Papa Maynard, she told him, said oxygen production alone
could not help Gaia, that the result could only be
further destabilization of the ecosystem. After the
firestorms began, few could disagree with the AI
anymore. Yet, wasn't Project Eden aimed at just
that—producing more oxygen? How could it
work?

He shook himself and started moving again. No.
Fusion washing was also supposed to make a lot
of water. That must be the difference. "Let the sweet
waters flow."

"It gives me the creeps," Whalen repeated in his
memory. Griffin repressed a shudder and turned down
the corridor toward Phoenix Company's quarters.

Chapter Twenty-One

The door to Hawkins' room was open, and he was playing a game of foursquare. When Griffin cleared his throat, he clicked off the images and looked up, smiling.

"Morning, guy. You're up early."

"So are you."

"Had trouble sleeping," said Hawkins.

"Bad dreams?"

Hawkins raised his eyebrows in surprise. "Funny question to ask. You know what? I didn't have *any* dreams. Almost seems like that's what kept waking me up, like I was looking for them and couldn't find any."

Griffin felt frozen for a moment, then shook it away.

"So, what's up?" said Hawkins.

Griffin told him the bad news about Kansas City and relayed Castle's message. Hawkins sat up straight; his smile dropped.

"Oh, brother. Thanks for letting me know. You said they're in the mess hall?"

"Were a few minutes ago. Just came in, so I expect they're still there."

Hawkins stood and sighed deeply. "I knew some folks in K.C. Did they say if anyone got out before the firestorm hit?"

"Well, a lot of folks had already cleared out of the whole area, but I don't know if there was a last-minute evac."

Hawkins nodded and walked past Griffin, his normally calm face tight and sad. Everybody in the platoon knew what a firestorm did—they'd gone through that in training. It was horrible.

Griffin's Militerm was flashing as he walked into his room, announcing mail. Griffin hesitated, afraid it might be Jenny. He tapped for the sender.

"Griffin, Barbara," the display said.

Griffin took a deep breath and sat down, his hands on either side of the terminal.

Her soft face was creased. He could see the line between her eyebrows that only showed when she was tired. She smiled.

"Hi! It's me. Listen—I'm sorry about my letter yesterday. I didn't mean to upset you like that. They tell you that you're supposed to know what you're going to say before you start recording. I swear, no matter how hard I try, I just can't do that. It all makes sense before I start and then when I begin, I don't remember what I wanted to say."

She paused, obviously searching for the right words.

"Anyway, I am sorry about yesterday. It was your father's birthday . . . or it would have been."

Griffin remembered the day his father died. He'd been late getting to the hospital, and when he walked into the room he saw that the bed was empty. His mother had put her hand to her forehead, then looked at him, and said, "He's gone, Andrew." He'd been surprised by his own grief. And by his anger.

"So I was just upset about that. He would be so proud of you, Drew."

She leaned forward, looking into her screen as though trying to catch his eye. "Please come home to me safe and sound. Drew, you're all I have left. Your father's gone, your sister's working for that damn lab—please, I need for you to come home to me."

She sighed, and he wished he could touch her, tell her to stop worrying, to stop pretending that he was something other than he was. He couldn't be her salvation. He couldn't even save himself.

"The other day I was watching the news and there was—"

Her face disappeared and the screen filled with a text announcement.

"The Office of Communication Management is

sorry to inform you that, under the authority of the Indentured Forces Act, we have found it necessary to edit this letter. We apologize for this necessity, but the correspondence was found to contain either inflammatory, confidential, secret, or otherwise jeopardizing information. Should you feel this letter was censored erroneously, you may file a formal protest with the Office of Communication Management."

"What is this crap?" Griffin stood and shouted at it as though it might answer. "What the hell could my own mother possibly say that would be some big deep secret!" The message just stared at him, solid and unbelievable.

He slapped off the offending blurb and began stalking back and forth. He hadn't really wanted to listen to his mother, she made him feel too guilty, reminded him too much of everything that he had loved, and mangled, and run away from. But now that the image was lost he felt bereft. She would have told him at the end that she loved him. Why couldn't those jerks have at least left that part in?

He stormed out of the room and began circling the second floor hall. His boots rang out on the Spectrastone paving as he stomped his way past the doors and corridors.

It didn't make any sense. They had censored Mom just as she was starting to talk about the news. She was OK but something big must have happened. Was Militerm keeping army folks from knowing about what was going on back home? Why was that?

Central processing was one floor up. Maybe he could get some answers there, depending on the interface. Militerm was set up for simple data retrieval and couldn't handle much in the way of queries.

Griffin took the lift up from enlisted quarters. The CP was directly above, so he had less chance of running into anyone. He didn't know if the third floor was off limits. With his luck, it was and he would run into Captain Zhorchow.

He hesitated at the lift exit, glanced both ways down the curving corridor and saw no one. It looked like every other floor in this base. Why couldn't they at least make the various areas different colors? It would help people find their way around. Of course, maybe the designers didn't care about helping people find things.

The door opened in front of him, and he entered a long, narrow room so crammed with displays and other equipment that he didn't immediately notice the man sitting at the main terminal. He hadn't expected anything on this order of magnitude. Military outposts didn't usually have even one Series 43 computer, and he could see control panels for at least three without even trying hard. This place had enough power to do major climate modeling. If the control system matched, there was no way his small skills would get him anywhere inside it.

"Estimate completion time frame, please."

A huge face appeared, green but nearly human in appearance and fully three dimensional. APs took their faces and bodies from human models. This image had a smooth wholeness that suggested it was being generated in real time. He was nearly certain this was entirely generated. Damn! What an interface this guy's got! That's a genuine artificial intelligence, the kind of entity that you didn't control so much as petition for cooperation.

"Assuming no supply shortfall, six weeks, three days," it said. Then it turned its bodiless face to look straight into his eyes.

"There is an unauthorized presence in the control room."

The man looked up, saw Griffin, and gave him an exasperated look.

"Private Griffin," said the artificial intelligence. "Do you have authorized business here?"

Griffin flinched, feeling the power of the thing's personality like a lash across his back.

"I want to protest a censorship," he said, putting his shoulders back. "My mother sent me a letter and—"

"Oh, really, Griffin, get a grip," the technician said. "If you're unhappy, protest to Communications." He crossed his arms.

"This area is restricted," the AI said. "You must

leave now please."

The thing was almost more daunting when it tried to be polite. Griffin backed up a step, then turned to leave. *This whole damn base is a restricted area. If they trust us so little, why don't they just lock us in our quarters?*

He took the lift downstairs and began circling the second floor, marching angrily through the empty corridors. He wanted to *do* something. The enlisted lounge was empty and the mess hall didn't smell good. He went back to his billet and paced impatiently. *Another thing to put on the "strange stuff" list,* he thought. *Kansas City dead. His mother's mail censored. Michaels and his underloaded mechanics and his VR drugs.* It made him itch.

He thought about querying Whalen's door, then decided against it. Despite their conversation last night, they had never been close—and at times like this, Hawkins was the best medicine the woman could get, Hawkins with his quiet strength and sustaining sympathy. But there *was* something he could do, he thought, and reached behind the books for the glass.

It looked unchanged from the night before. He carefully emptied the water out and dropped the glass in the recycler, then put the flower in his pocket and headed for sick bay.

Chapter Twenty-Two

D r. Mirren wasn't in, but he didn't really want to see her. Instead, he lounged against the nurse's desk, waiting for Marie Lukas to finish tapping something into her computer. He remembered doing this sort of thing during his internship, in the few minutes he would have between trauma unit catastrophes. Leaning against the nursing station, shooting the bull with the overworked nurses, with the other interns, with Jenny. Gallows humor to cope with the sea of human misery that washed over them every shift.

He and Jenny had once made the mistake of telling some of those jokes at the dinner table when his mother had come to visit, and she had been shocked. "How can you joke about people dying of thirst?" Barbara Griffin demanded. "Or of environmental poisons? That's—that's horrible!"

Jenny had reached across the table and captured Barbara's hands in her own. "Because if we don't laugh, we'll start crying, Barb," she had said earnestly. "And if we start crying, we may never be able to stop."

Griffin shook the memory away abruptly as Marie turned from the computer and looked at him.

"You got a good excuse for being here?" she demanded. "Or you lookin' for a shot?"

"Hey, peace, it's me, remember? The ex-med student?" He grinned at her. "I just want to examine your—equipment."

Marie laughed, the first full-bodied laugh he had heard in ages.

"Boy, you have got some guts," she said. "Either that, or you don't have the brains God gave a fish. What you want with me?"

"No, I really do want to look at the equipment," Griffin said. "I mean, much as I might want to, Nurse Lukas, I have far too much respect for you to mess with you. Honest." He leered at her, and she grinned.

"OK, what?" she said.

Griffin walked across the sickbay. "It's this thing," he said. "The Jensen Ultra. They were just about to get one at the hospital when I—uh, joined up. I've been curious about them. Can I take a look?"

"Not with your own hands you don't," she said, and came across to him. "You got any idea how much these babies cost? Here, I'll show you."

Perfect, he thought, as the machine hummed to

life. He waited until the hum filled the area, then touched her shoulder and, when she looked at him, he put the lily in her hand. She looked startled.

"It's from the atrium," he said under the sound of the machine. "Can you run a scan on it?"

She didn't move, and for a moment he wondered if he had miscalculated, if Marie Lukas was in on whatever was going on here, if she'd turn him in. She looked at him steadily and he forced himself to look back, then she nodded and closed her fingers around the flower.

"Tomorrow," she said, as quietly as he was speaking. "I'll have to juggle, but I think I can do it. You want a full scan?"

"I don't know," he said. "I want to know what it's made of."

She slid the flower into her uniform pocket, and powered down the Jensen Ultra.

"There," she said. "That's pretty much all there is to it except for the programming end. And if you think I'm letting you get near the code, soldier boy—"

"No, no." Griffin raised his hands, palms out. "I wouldn't dream of it. Thank you, Nurse Lukas. You've been very helpful."

"You get going before I get my syringe," she said, hands on hips, and Griffin backed quickly out of sickbay, his hands firmly on his ass. He could hear her laughter as the door closed between them.

Chapter Twenty-Three

Hawkins was still with Whalen. Griffin went in search of Michaels and finally found him in the simulation room, deep into it, his body moving smooth and hard through whatever reality was going on under his TopHat. Griffin paused to watch him for a moment. Say what you would about the man, when it came to fighting he was absolutely brilliant. Griffin envied his ability to turn everything off except for the moment, the present, the now. It was, Michaels had explained sarcastically, a freaking gift.

Then Griffin heard the sarge and Andrews talking at the far end of the room and slipped out before they saw him. He'd put in his two hours later, he thought.

Coming out of the room, he remembered the conversation between Dr. Marks and the colonel he'd overheard the day before and thought about his own conversation with her over breakfast this morning. Alonzo was right—she was beautiful. And Charlie Becker was right—she was intelligent. And his own gut instinct was right—she was in trouble.

Drag twelve billion people through—the Gate? Where could they possibly put twelve billion people on Planet AJ3905, with its fatal atmosphere and its deadly bugs?

Griffin took a deep breath. Maybe Dr. Marks was in enough trouble that she would be willing to make a deal—maybe they could help each other. At the very least, maybe she could tell him what was going on.

He went down the corridor until he came to the civilian lab, where Dr. Marks worked. After a moment of hesitation, he stepped forward. Somewhat to his surprise, the door opened without a security lockout, and he went in.

A short hallway led into a broad open room, with a wall full of displays that he couldn't read. Were they decorations or data? Difficult to tell when you had no idea what was going on.

Dr. X. I. Li, Dr. Marks' assistant, looked at a moving display and made notes on a folio computer. Her smooth hair glistened in the changing light. The data appeared to be about plants.

"Hello," she said. "Put them on the desk there. Thank you."

Griffin smiled, looking at her crisp profile against the lighted displays. "I beg your pardon?"

"Put them on the desk." She did not look away from her notes, and her crisp voice was impatient.

"I'm sorry. I don't know what you're talking about."

"What—" She looked at him. "Oh! I'm sorry. I thought you were . . . I'm sorry. May I help you?"

"Uh, maybe. Is Dr. Marks here?"

She just looked at him.

"I mean, I talked to her earlier, and she seemed a little—" Griffin waved his hand, unwilling to put a name on how Dr. Marks had seemed. "I just thought I'd see if she was OK. Is she? OK, I mean?"

"Dr. Marks is not here," the woman said curtly. "You are not allowed to be in here. This is a restricted area." Her face became stern. "You need to go."

"Look, you don't have to get uptight about it. I just wanted to know—"

"Please leave now," Dr. Li said, rising. "I do not want to have to report you. The UN is very strict about security areas."

Griffin felt his temper start to fray. "Then why wasn't your door secure?" he demanded.

"I was expecting a delivery," she said. "I am still expecting a delivery. Please leave. Now." She looked at him flatly, her arms loose at her side. For a moment, she reminded him of Cranshaw.

Griffin left, muttering. He wasn't upset at being

tossed out of the laboratory as much as he was at the woman's attitude. Dr. Marks *was* in trouble. She *was* having a hard time. And her assistant didn't seem worried at all.

Chapter Twenty-Four

Outside the civilian lab, Griffin tapped at a Militerm and checked the time, then sighed. He was scheduled for sim training, and as much as he didn't want to, he'd better get his two hours in.

Hawkins was there, talking quietly but urgently to Sarge. Griffin nodded, and passed by closely enough to hear that they were talking about Whalen, and that Sarge knew the woman was taking Compassionate Leave for the day. Griffin sat, put on the TopHat, and gritted his teeth through the uncomfortable moments of transition until the shunts were firmly in place. An information display scrolled in front of him, stuff about rules and regs and not loitering in the mess hall—all the garbage that some officer was probably paid lots of money to write, and which nobody read unless they absolutely had to. Griffin had read it all before and, as it scrolled by, noted that nothing had changed.

Then he heard Michaels speak as though right next to him.

"Come on out of the database. It's time to rock and roll, baby boy!"

The information display vanished, to be replaced by that poisonous looking sky. Griffin felt his heart rate accelerate almost instantly.

The simulation was even more intense than yesterday. He'd never gone so deep into a VR in his life. He completely lost awareness that he was inside an artificial universe. When three bugs attacked him at once and killed him, he woke up inside the TopHat's readouts deeply shocked and disoriented. Strange stuff.

Also very satisfying. As he checked his kill rate, he realized he had felt positively exultant each time the death scream of a bug sounded. He *wanted* to kill bugs. The thought of actually going outside and doing it for real made his skin tingle.

Sarge did a postmortem on the run, reamed him out heavy for letting his skivver be boxed in, and then he was back into it for another run. He hated the bugs; he hated the very ground they crawled on. He loved getting over them and raining fire down on their wriggling bodies. The hideous sky twisted over his head as he screamed joy at the deaths below him.

After the fifth run, Sarge said, "Time for a break." For a moment he was outright angry with her. He wanted to go back into sim, to spend the rest of the day doing this simple and lovely job of erasing bugs from Johnson's Archipelago.

As he took off the helmet and stood, he reminded himself repeatedly that it had all been a sort of dream, not reality at all. Reality would be different. If he got jumped by a bug out there, he wouldn't wake up inside a quiet suit sitting on a soft chair. He'd be dead. Pure and simple. Dead.

He left the room and found himself standing in the corridor, still dazed. Hawkins put a hand on his shoulder, looked him in the eyes, and then passed on by. Castle, Alonzo, Michaels, and Hynick left in a clump, arguing fiercely about the last maneuver and apparently headed upstairs, to waste their half-hour break over the poisonous coffee in the mess hall. Hynick must have been observing. He hadn't been a member of the run.

Part of him wanted to be killing bugs in sim. And another part of him was starting to rear up its head in horror at his inability to pull back fully from the VR. He suddenly needed very much to be alone for a moment, and he punched the lift for the first floor, went down the corridor to the airlock, and found the atrium door.

Griffin sat on the nearest bench, watching that lovely bright light. It was good to feel the warmth, the heavy sweetness of the air, and the slightly damp bench underneath him. Slowly the feeling of horror drained away. Michaels had to be right—Griffin couldn't be the person who screamed in joy at the death of the aliens. He had never liked inflicting death.

He closed his eyes and concentrated, moving away from the emotions and into a quiet place, a place where he could reach serenity. His shoulders started to relax, and the warmth and peace of the atrium helped. Jenny would like this place.

His interior peace shattered and his hands clenched down on themselves. Hard. Jenny. That terrible fight.

His mother had called him an hour after Jenny's accident.

"Drew, there's been an accident."

He knew right away it was Jenny. He knew it was his fault. The collision control system on that car had been flaky for months and he'd never said anything about it. An accident. A bad one, or his mother would have told him first that Jenny was OK. Jenny was not OK. Jenny would never be OK again.

His mother's concerned face looked into his from the projection screen and her voice droned on. He didn't hear the words but absorbed the terrible content.

When Jenny got really angry, she would go roaring down old-fashioned back roads. Very few people frequented those roads and fewer still had malfunctioning collision detectors. If the other car's had worked, it wouldn't have happened. A head-on with both cars going over fifty miles an hour. Plasticsteel and webs could only do so much. The driver of the other car had died instantly. If the next person on the scene had not been a nurse, Jenny would have died too.

His mother didn't know what Jenny's injuries were, just that she had been badly burned but was still alive. Mom told him where the hospital was and signed off, obviously expecting him to meet her there.

Instead, Griffin had sat in front of the whited out screen for nearly an hour, his mind a riot of images. He had failed. He always failed. He put on a good show at first, didn't he? Everyone would be so impressed with him in the beginning. And then he would start messing it up.

He'd been messing up medical school the day Jenny picked him up in that entertainment mall. For her, he had pulled it together and gotten his undergraduate work done only a year late. He'd been happy. She'd been proud of him. But that had changed this past year, hadn't it? He started messing up again. Not because it was hard, not because he didn't want to please her. He didn't know why. He just had.

Now he had messed up again, big time, and Jenny's lovely body was mangled.

Without knowing precisely what he was going

to do, he packed a suitcase, put on his nose filters and goggles, and walked out of the apartment they had shared. He took nothing that he couldn't carry. He walked. And walked. And walked. Then he walked into a bright and jazzy bar, and got himself blitzed.

He wasn't sure why he had joined Beatrice three days later. Still, where else did a coward belong? Someone who couldn't face his responsibilities? Who ran out on his beloved in her time of need? The military was perfect for him. Do what you're told. No responsibility. No worries. No failure.

A lift began its whine down from second to first, and he snapped out of his painful reverie. Alonzo and Hynick made obscene gestures at the Venus de Milo statue behind him. He rolled his eyes and went back to the sim bay.

Chapter Twenty-Five

They did ground maneuvers for another hour, deathly boring except for the occasional bug kills. He liked skivvers better, even in simulation. Walking around waiting for something to jump out at you wasn't his idea of fun. Sarge called a lunch break.

"I don't know what's gotten into you guys. Never seen grunts so eager to do training." She shook her head, looking both puzzled and pleased. "Had to pry Castle away last night—she was doing a long sim run and it was time for lights out. Keep it up and you might actually get passable at this."

Lunch was spaghetti. It smelled almost right, but the pasta was overcooked and the sauce was thin. He didn't feel like talking so he took the plate to his room.

No new mail. Good. Each time the message light lit, he feared more deeply that it would be Jenny. He hadn't seen her since the fight, since before she took off and had the accident. There were some photos in the medical records he'd hacked into, but he hadn't called them up. The hologram MRI was more than he could stand as it was.

He set the plate on his desk and, for the first time since joining Beatrice, he composed a short message to his mother. He kept having to back up and start over again. The knowledge that it would be viewed by other people and maybe censored before she ever saw it made him self-conscious and angry. He kept thinking of more and more things he would like to tell her, things about fusion scrubbing, and Planet AJ3905, and the anguish on Dr. Marks's face, and the light in the atrium that was so right that it was wrong. He knew he couldn't say any of it. But the one thing that wouldn't be censored was the thing he still couldn't bring himself to say—that he was tired of running away. That he was tired of turning his back on the problems in his life.

That he was sorry.

So he sent her a short, unconvincing note, full of platitudes and skimpy on details, and knew that this stupid note, with his stupid face and his stupid grin, would become one of her treasures. Because it was the first time he'd sent anything.

He only hoped, for her sake, that he didn't look as ashamed as he felt.

After returning his plate to the mess hall, Griffin

reported back to the briefing room. The second set of simulation runs was even more intense than the first. And, once again, he went so deeply into sim that he didn't wonder at his joy in the work, he just perfected his skills at finding bugs and sneaking up on them.

Sarge pulled him and Michaels out early.

"Time for KP, boys." She smiled at Michaels. He looked back at her without expression. "Oh, Michaels—grow up. You've been in the army a long time. You mouth off, you get KP."

Michaels' mouth twitched in a small smile and he nodded. "OK, boss lady. But don't expect me to stop complaining about those suits."

"I'd be a fool to expect you to stop complaining about anything. Just keep it down in the public places. Ask me for a meeting. You know I'll listen, don't you?"

Michaels just looked at her. Griffin suddenly remembered his conversation with Private Lopez the night before. Michaels and the sarge? They neither said nor did anything that might lead to that impression, but Griffin couldn't shake the feeling that Lopez was right.

"Yes, ma'am," Michaels finally said.

"OK, get that place clean. And while you're at it, teach Cookie how to make things taste a little better."

"I'll do my best," said Michaels.

They headed up in the lift.

Cookie glared at Michaels when they came in and wordlessly led them to a set of troughs in the back of the cafeteria. Michaels must have been charming the locals again. The sad-faced man pointed and said, "Make 'em shine" and left them looking at the thick black slime lining an array of semicircular metal containers. Griffin didn't know what they were used for, but it couldn't be good.

Michaels pulled an odd-looking gadget off a rack behind them and opened it, revealing a set of paddles that had nearly the same diameter at the troughs. Trust Michaels to have run into this job before. Griffin watched him for a minute, then pulled another tool off the wall and took it to the farthest trough. Michaels still looked abstracted. With any luck at all, they would be done before he was ready to talk and Griffin wouldn't have to hear what he had to say.

They worked in smelly silence for nearly an hour before Michaels finally spoke. Griffin was thinking about the last simulation run when he noticed that the burly man had stopped working and was looking at him.

"What, have I developed a second head?" he said.

"I saw Whalen at breakfast today. She looked pretty bad."

Griffin nodded. "Yeah. Kansas City bought it. You wouldn't think there was enough oxygen left for that kind of fire to keep going."

"Won't be much longer. Those UN jerk offs have stopped messing with the Gulf, so the big oxy surge is backing off. You'd think the ozone blast in '52 would have convinced them to quit messing with the atmosphere, but no. They've got to do it again. And now we're supposedly helping them with another one of their idiot experiments."

The words were typical Michaels, but the tone wasn't. He didn't sound like he was paying much attention to what he was saying.

"OK, what is it?"

Michaels actually focused on him. "It? Man, what are you talking about?"

"Whatever it is you've got on that lump of gray shit you call a brain."

"I don't know, man. I don't think this is the place to talk about it."

"Damn it, Michaels, cut it out!" Griffin slapped his paddles against the trough. "If you've got something to say, say it! I'm tried of all this yes-and-no, cloak-and-dagger shit. What the hell is wrong?"

He expected Michaels to blow his top, yell, and that would be the end of it. Instead, Michaels just looked at him.

"The UN is lying to us," he said finally. "Again. We're not on AJ3905, or whatever the hell they say this is. There is no Johnson's Archipelago, at least not here. There are no bugs. I don't know what we're shooting at, but it's not whatever the UN says it is."

"Ah, shit," Griffin said, not wanting to hear it. "I just thought you were thinking about boinking the sarge."

Michaels stared at him for a moment, then shook his head. "You are a piece of work," he said. "Is that all you can think about? I tell you, they're lying, and it's not just for practice."

Griffin stared back at him. The cold feeling in his stomach was so bad he wanted to double over or throw up. Or run. Instead, he clutched the paddles. "Goddamn it, Michaels, I think you've finally bought it," he said furiously. "You know what? I don't want to know."

"They're planning to blow your ass up, and you don't care?"

"And you don't know! Just shut up, Michaels. You don't know shit!"

Michaels shook his head, and suddenly the tension broke.

"And even if I did know shit, you wouldn't want to hear about it," he said amiably, and flicked open his paddles. "Griffie, I just hope you have a chance to grow up before you die."

Griffin looked at him for a few seconds, filled with frustration, curiosity, and a deep wish that all the mysteries would stop. To hell with Michaels. To hell with paranoid theories. To hell with all of it.

Besides, Michaels wouldn't take the argument

personally. He never did. It was, perhaps, the most frustrating thing about him.

They worked for another half hour in silence, and then one of the APs appeared.

"Survey Team Gamma report to the egress chamber. Alonzo, Alvarez, Michaels, and Tisch report to the egress chamber please."

Michaels straightened from his work and smiled at the patch of wall where the figure had been.

"You'd do *anything* to get out of KP, wouldn't you?" said Griffin.

Michaels put the cleaner back onto its hook, stretched, and grinned. "You bet your pretty blues. See ya later, man."

"Break a leg," Griffin said to his retreating back as he swaggered out of the room.

Chapter Twenty-Six

Cookie shooed him out a half hour later, and got huffy when Griffin asked what was for dinner.

"It'll be good this time, you just wait and see. Takes real talent to make specialized diets work right. This place messes up what you boys need to eat, and that's why things haven't been tasting right. But I'll show you what I can do, you just wait and see."

Griffin walked out while the man was still muttering, and could hear him railing right up until the door closed. Guy didn't really need an audience, he was just as happy performing for himself.

Griffin stood in the corridor, wondering what to do next. He had nothing scheduled until dinner, and he really doubted that would be better than any other meal he'd had here. Maybe another simulation run? If Gamma Team was out on survey, there might be slots available in the bay. The idea of going under the helmet again was appealing. It was so simple, so certain. All he thought about was finding and killing bugs—no confusions about astonishingly powerful AIs or high-level UN SciTechs acting weird.

The thought of sim was *so* attractive it made him feel a little frightened. Sarge thought it was strange how hot for training they all were. So did he.

Instead, he stopped by the enlisted lounge, hoping for something to help distract him. The room was beautiful, maybe even more so than the atrium. Great holographic skyscapes of changing forms covered the ceilings and walls, and floating spinning balls much like planets drifting through the air. If you wanted, you could play with the balls, either by just batting them around or by getting up a game of skyball.

Charlie Becker, the Quantum Gate tech, sat alone at a table, scribbling madly into a bound book. Charlie Becker had said he didn't know how the Gate could possibly work. Griffin hesitated, then went over.

"Hey," he said. "Mind if I sit with you?"

The tech blinked at him, as if he'd never seen Griffin before, and clutched the journal to his chest.

"No!" he said. "No, no, this is important, you know, this is my soul, this is where I reveal the most intimate secrets of my innermost—" He stopped abruptly and blinked at Griffin through his impossibly thick lenses. "It's the only place," he said. "You'd think she'd understand that, but she doesn't. All she cares about is rank, rank and all that big-time brass kind of stuff and she doesn't even see me. Oh, but she will, yes indeed, she certainly will, uh huh. Because I've got plans, big plans, for her, you know." He blinked at Griffin again, then slammed the book closed and leaped to his feet.

"You can't chase me out of here!" he yelled as he rushed through the door and down the hall.

Griffin gaped after him, and in the far corner, John DiSilva looked up from the insides of an old clock shaped like a cartoon mouse.

"Man's insane," he said, and puffed at a huge cigar.

Griffin thought about Dr. Marks and her cigarettes, and was about to ask DiSilva about it when the mechanic put his screwdriver inside the clock and twisted. The hands of the clock, each tipped with a white glove, flew across the room.

Griffin turned and left, but before he could reach enlisted quarters, an alarm went off. An AP appeared on the wall next to him.

"Level one alert. Level one alert. Rescue Team A report immediately to the egress chamber. Andrews, Cranshaw, Griffin, and Hawkins report immediately to the egress chamber."

Griffin headed out, his heart hammering. He dove into the lift, and the whine as it went down seemed unusually loud. Were they going to go outside?

The hangar had been dead silent when he visited yesterday. Now the air vibrated with the sounds of outriggers being pumped and loaders moving equipment.

The door to the skivver irised open as he approached, its Plasticsteel rippling apart in a smooth oval. He could hear Sarge's voice inside. He stopped in front of the door, reluctant to go inside. *Now it begins.* This had to be a mission. The bilious skies of AJ3905 flickered in his mind's eye. *Oh, man, no—I do not want to go out there.* He took a deep breath and climbed aboard.

Cranshaw, Andrews, and Hawkins were already clustered around the briefing display table in the long blue room of the main hold. Andrews had shed his UN officer's monkey suit for working clothes. A generated map glowed on the table as Cranshaw and Andrews spoke. It was the first area map that Griffin had seen and he craned his neck, wishing he could see it more clearly.

Andrews turned away from his study of the maps. "Listen up! A survey team has been attacked in sector A-twelve. The skivver's down and we have fatalities. It looks like we're dealing with a new type of bug, and these fly."

Griffin kept his face still but his guts clenched. Bugs that could fly? The ones they'd been fighting in sim were a major threat to foot patrols and could leap high enough to attack a low-flying skivver, but all the tactics they'd been learning were based on the idea that you could lift up and bomb them into extinction.

"We're downloading the flight recorder playback simulation now. We're going to need the first aid kit, oxygen, and body bags. Sergeant—who's your best driver?"

"Griffin." She looked at Griffin flatly. "You've got the bubble on this one."

He nodded.

Cranshaw said, "I need a wireframe!"

The on-board systems replied with an elevation map that appeared in the middle of the briefing table. Like most elevations, it was great for contour and piss-poor for anything else. Where *were* they?

"Damn! They would be on the other side of the island. We'll skirt the fault line," she pointed at a long line near the center of the island, "and crank up the sensors when we hit the south perimeter of A-twelve."

Griffin blinked. What are they doing way over there? What could there be left to survey, anyway? The island just wasn't that big. Overfly it a couple of times and a reconstruction ought to tell you everything you needed to know about this poisonous rock.

An AP appeared beside the map. "Playback

ready."

The elevation map vanished and the playback came up, inscribed as 11/26/57 PacTrans Extrapolate. The skivver was in the air, surrounded by at least a dozen flying bugs who seemed to be worrying at it. A voice said, "Damn it! We're losing pillow!" Sounded like Tisch.

The skivver had lost *pillow*? Gaia! What did the bugs do? How could that happen without an engine blowout or electronic interference? Was that the same mission Michaels had gone out on earlier?

The skivver tilted, then headed for the side of a hill. Just before it slammed into the hill, the bugs scattered in all directions. The main body of the skivver remained intact through the crash, but it lost an outrigger against the rocks and dirt. Watching the impact made Griffin's stomach hurt, imagining himself inside and being bounced around. A crash siren was howling in the background. As if anyone in that skivver had needed an alarm to tell them they were crashing. The playback ended.

Cranshaw's voice snapped his attention to her. "Everybody—full side arms. Lock and load. Griffin, we need you at the helm, please."

As he headed toward the front cabin, Andrews held out a hand.

"Private Griffin, these things brought down a skivver. . . ."

No shit, Griffin thought angrily, I hadn't noticed.
"So set your gyro sensitivity to minimum."

Griffin blinked at Andrews for a moment. Gyros? What makes you think gyros would help if the electronics are getting hosed?

"Yes, sir," he said and continued toward the controls.

Chapter Twenty-Seven

Hawkins, you're on the auxiliary," Cranshaw said.

"Hey, no problem!"

Thank God it's Hawkins, thought Griffin as he started the flight sequence. His weapons scores were nearly as high as Michaels'.

The skivver's light painted the inside of the hangar in alternating red and white as the outriggers were lowered into position. Griffin watched the connections closely from the camera feed. Maybe the previous skivver hadn't had a solid load. Five sets of clamps snugged down perfectly, and a quick glow indicated EM glue activation. Nothing wrong there.

"Outrigger attached. Skivver ready to depart," said an AP. A different AP appeared and said, "The P.A.I. has calculated an optimal flight plan. It's logged and approved. You have a two-kilometer variance zone."

Griffin punched for the take-off macro. The skivver vibrated under him, then rose, pivoted, and moved out through the dense energy curtain of the exit hatch.

Griffin's heart rose as the skivver headed up into the strange sky. The craft handled like a dream under his hands, moving quickly and responsively through the air. Even across such ugly terrain and toward such uncertain risks, flying was a joy. He'd always been good with planes, helis, and skivvers. Jenny joked that he was most at home without his feet on the ground.

He soared past brown and scrofulous hills, carefully maintaining the course laid in by the on-board while checking for any changes in the land beneath them. His console display was breaking up periodically, producing bursts of static that almost hurt his brain with their intensity. The grays would flash to an odd green and then back to the usual rolling hills. He slapped the console a couple times, but it didn't seem to make any difference. He logged a maintenance request for the mechanic to check it out next cycle.

Just past the tall spike of a mountain, the skivver's AP set off an alarm and said, "Alien proximity unacceptable." A flying bug rounded the hill and launched itself at them.

The bug was huge, with a wingspan that covered his display and clawed legs waving wildly as it swooped down at him. It was black with hints of green and large yellow eyes. The targeting square came up and he fired. The bug screamed and flashed into white for a heartbeat, but kept coming. It was vaguely humanoid in shape, with two long arms outspread, from which spiky wings fanned out. It looked almost as if it intended to embrace the skivver. Three legs dangled loosely beneath its shiny body. Hawkins lined up on it and made the shot.

The bug exploded like a plastic toy, jagged pieces flying through the air. Griffin heard a few thumps against the hull of the skivver and then they were past. He'd seen it happen this way in sim but now it struck him as weird. Even Earth insects had a circulatory system of some sort. What kind of living creature simply came apart when shot with a laser rifle? Stranger still, he'd felt a flicker of grief at seeing it blow up. The exaltation he'd come to associate with bug kills from the sim runs hit after a heart beat, but something inside still felt *sorry* for the bug.

The AP said, "I have a lock on Dr. Marks's skivver."

Dr. *Marks*?

The skivver came into sight beneath them. The wreck didn't look nearly as bad as it had from the PacTrans. One of the outriggers lay at a fair distance from the main body, but it otherwise looked like it could just take off. He had expected a burn across the soil and dented equipment. Griffin swung around the site in a quick circle, looking for other bugs nearby, but saw only the rough brown dirt. He set the skivver down carefully.

"I show three fatalities," said the AP, "an injury, and a clean survive. The injury and the survive are in the skivver's EO-two station."

Griffin started to get up from his console but Cranshaw waved him back. "Griffin, stay on the cannons. Let's go, Hawkins. I'll take the living, you take the dead."

"Yes, Sergeant," said Hawkins and they both disappeared into the back of the skivver. After they'd donned their suits, the airlock cycled them out onto the surface. The VR display showed them as moving circles, Cranshaw in blue and Hawkins in red. The red dot moved toward a much smaller dot labeled "Alonzo." Not far away was another that said "Tisch." The size of the dots showed that both were dead.

Tisch was dead! So it *had* been his voice on the PacTrans replay. While he waited to hear the airlock cycle out, Griffin remembered the night five of them had snuck out past the guards to see an illegal stick game going down twenty-five kilometers away. It had been Michaels' idea, of course. They had gotten into trouble for it. Tisch more than the rest of them—he'd found a friendly lady and been later than the rest getting back. Cranshaw had talked the C.O. out of giving him brig time, and had a chat with Tisch later that left the man white. He never did repeat what Sarge had said, but Griffin had the feeling he might have preferred the brig to getting chewed out by Cranshaw.

Cranshaw's voice jumped him back into the present. "I've got the two live ones. Michaels is fine. Alvarez's suit is breached, but it looks patchable."

"A second-tier patch may prove sufficient," said an AP.

"Got it. Installing patch."

"I'm seeing two DOAs," said Hawkins, "but no sign of Dr. Marks."

"I am experiencing some interference with the location of Dr. Marks's body," said the AP and Griffin looked at the calm female face in astonishment. How could it be unable to find a dead body? What about the transponders? His instruments weren't showing any unusual EM. What else could cause such a problem? "I will continue filtering for location. VR feed will occur if I'm successful. In the meantime, please recover the locatable bodies."

"Coming in," said Cranshaw.

The rear airlock opened, closed, and cycled. Griffin swiveled his pilot's chair so he could see the entry. As the decontamination units hissed, Andrews unrolled several pallets. He stood by with a combat first aid kit, looking tense and restless.

The door opened. Cranshaw and Michaels had

already peeled off their CO suits and helmets. They were pulling Alvarez free of his suit while getting him through the door. They kicked it away and half-carried him into the main room.

Andrews scrambled forward. "Get him down." he said, gesturing toward the nearest pallet.

"Easy, easy!" said Cranshaw as she and Michaels lowered the gasping man.

"On-board!" said Andrews, "Get me a StatScan." He knelt on the floor and opened his kit.

"Scanning, sir."

"Watch his head!" said Cranshaw. "I'll get the helmet." The latches had already been undone with the removal of the CO suit, and it slid off easily, revealing Alvarez's face twisted with pain.

The airlock door irised briefly again, and Hawkins came in dragging two limp suited figures by their helmet loops. Griffin swallowed hard, watching him lay the dead men gently on the floor.

Michaels started shouting. Shocked, Griffin turned his head and saw the man haul Andrews to his feet by one arm.

"Damn it! You bastards!" He turned and grabbed Andrews. "Did you know about the SD devices?" Michaels' face was twisted with rage and fear.

Griffin rose from his chair and started toward them, not sure what was going on or what he could do.

"Get off me!" shouted Andrews and shook off

his grip.

Cranshaw barked, "Michaels! Step down."

Michaels pointed at Alonzo. "Look! These men were euthanized!" He grabbed Andrews' arm again. "You killed them!"

Chapter Twenty-Eight

Griffin felt his skin chill and his face go white. SD? *Self-destruct*? They put self-destruct devices into our suits?

Andrews jerked his arm free once more. "This man needs medical help now! If you don't want to kill him, you'll back off." He pushed Michaels away and knelt beside Alvarez.

Michaels reached for him again. Cranshaw moved in behind him, snaked her right arm under his, and clamped a hand against the back of his neck, forcing his head forward.

"Michaels!" she shouted, "Stand down!"

"Jesus! All right. Let go of me!" Michaels was breathing hard and so was Andrews.

An AP appeared and spoke into the brief silence. "Contusions. Shock. Recommend one hundred cc Meta-Alkaloid."

Alvarez's face was contorted and blood dripped slowly from his lower lip. "Can I get some medicine here please?" he said in a tight voice. Andrews plucked a spray syringe out of the kit and held it briefly against his jugular. Alvarez sighed and relaxed.

Cranshaw still had Michaels in the lock. "I said all right, goddamn it! Will you let go!"

From the look of it, Alvarez probably had at least one broken rib, in addition to the cut on his face. Obviously he'd bounced, hard, against something inside the skivver—according to the early flight report, neither Michaels nor Alvarez had gone outside at all.

Cranshaw slowly released Michaels, watching him narrowly. He stood and gestured toward the dead men again. "Look—Alonzo and Tisch were euthanized. The bugs didn't kill them! The UN did. Why weren't we told?"

The UN lieutenant was checking readouts on his handheld. Without looking up, Andrews responded, "The air of this rock is highly toxic. Do you have any idea what that soup out there does to a man? It was standard procedure, if it wasn't for the SDs those men would still be in agony. Or would you rather have seen that?"

"Hey, screw you, man! You could have told us. You don't go putting self-destruct devices on envirosuits without telling people. Why don't you go flatline!"

He stopped yelling, and the only sound in the

compartment was his ragged breathing. He began stripping off his gloves.

"Screw this. I am not fighting. And when I get back to the base, every swinging Dick and Jane on that base is gonna know about it. This is gonna make Rangoon look like a freaking ladies—"

Griffin hadn't even seen Sarge draw her gun, but now it was pointed at Michaels' face.

"You, Private Michaels, are in breach of contract and I'm afraid I am going to have to put you on notice." Her voice was very cold, very formal.

"Jesus Christ, Maria. Are you for real?"

Griffin sucked in air sharply. Sarge walked slowly toward Michaels, keeping the gun on him.

"Private Michaels, Beatrice International is hereby notifying you that you are in breach of your employment contract. Please do not call me by my first name."

"Notice is duly received." said Michaels. Griffin wasn't sure if he was taking Cranshaw seriously. By the expression on her face, he certainly should be.

She continued to approach him. "I am obligated to inform you that your contract is currently being interpreted under the Indentured Forces Act." The gun was now touching the man's chest. As he looked down at it, his face changed and he raised his hands. Griffin felt a wash of relief. Michaels knew she meant it.

"Failure to cure this breach," she said, and raised

her gun to his neck, "could result in substantial penalties." She pushed the gun's muzzle into the soft underside of Michaels' chin.

For a long still moment, Griffin was afraid she might blow Michaels' head off right in front of them. Please, no. Please don't do it. Griffin was afraid to breath. Michaels blinked. Cranshaw did not. She waited.

Finally, Michaels spoke again. His face was still angry, but his voice was almost amused. "I take your meaning . . . Maria."

Both of them maintained the same position for several moments more. Griffin knew that Michaels meant it, but he sure wished the guy hadn't insisted on first-naming her again. He could almost see her considering whether or not to accept this as acquiescence.

She did. She nodded and slowly pointed her gun toward the ceiling instead of at his face. Michaels stepped back from her and picked up his gloves. Under her watching eyes, he put them back on and went to help Hawkins tend to the bodies.

"Nicely done, Sergeant," said Andrews, sounding almost as surprised as he did respectful.

Cranshaw grimaced slightly and Griffin realized that she disliked Andrews. She nodded, then looked at Griffin.

"Private Griffin," she said, "get us home, please." The gun was still in her hand, safety off and aimed up. He wished she would put it away.

"Yeah," said Andrews. "Can we get the hell out of here, please?"

Griffin went to his console and set up for take-off.

"The bodies are in the hold," said Hawkins.

Griffin activated pillow and pulled back on the stick, grateful to get out of this place. He rose at top speed into the ugly sky, pushing away all the questions and fears with the wrecked survey skivver. They were still out on the surface of AJ3905, and there were still bugs in the area. He didn't want, for the moment, to think about what Sarge's orders were, or "substantial penalties," or any of it. Just fly. The dark landscape moved beneath him, now unbroken by the display malfunctions he'd seen on the way out. He felt a vague gratitude for the simplicity of this trip, then suppressed even that to focus on the feel of the machine and the play of the controls.

The squat octagonal base came into view, doors already open to bring the skivver in. Griffin turned control over to the on-board and let it take them through the shield curtain. He watched, feeling dead inside, as they settled into the bay, then ran through the shut-down sequence.

A mechanized gurney from sickbay was waiting in the hangar. Andrews and Michaels gently rolled Alvarez onto it. As they followed it out the door,

Griffin caught a glimpse of Michaels' face. Total blankness, the eyes distant and the face still. Not good, thought Griffin, what is he planning? Griffin shuddered once and pushed the thought aside as Michaels and Andrews left the hangar.

Hawkins was opening the hold doors. Griffin helped him get the still-suited bodies of the dead onto another gurney, this one broad and shrouded. They watched in silence as it rolled away. There would be services later. Griffin felt they ought to say something now—a salutation or a farewell—but his mind was blank. Hawkins sighed and the moment passed.

Sarge unloaded and checked out the remaining gear from the skivver. They went in to help. When the lists were completed and cleared through an AP, Griffin's next plan was to go to his room and bury himself in sleep, if possible. As he was headed out, Sarge called to him.

"I think Saunders is expecting you."

He nodded automatically and the door closed behind him. He stood in front of it, feeling both frightened and tired. Jeez. Saunders? He thought longingly of his room and his bunk.

He sighed, entered the lift, and pressed "Three." The lift rose up through the levels and layers of the atrium. Some of the trees were nearly as tall as the entire atrium, their straight trunks and feathery leaves rising through the air. The lift doors opened and he was once again in the dense sterile corridors of the base. When he palmed the door to Saunders' office, he had a moment's hope it wouldn't open.

The door irised open into a short dark hallway with big double doors at the end of it. The doors were covered with an angular green pattern that reminded him unpleasantly of a face. He walked toward it, feeling like he was about to be swallowed up. Music sounded, barely louder than his own footfalls on the smooth floor. The rich yet spare tones reminded him of some Baroque pieces he had once heard. The whole feeling was of foreboding elegance. The doors swung inward as he approached.

Chapter Twenty-Nine

Saunders sat at the far end of the room, behind a large round desk with the UN logo on top. Behind him glowed a piece of stained glass that had to be at least six meters high. The rich reds, greens, and blues would have looked more at home in a church. The pattern was symmetrical but abstract. Saunders leaned back in his chair before it, stroking his short, black beard. He should have looked dwarfed by the art behind him. He didn't.

Michaels and Andrews stood in front of the colonel, both as tense as if they were preparing for another brawl. Griffin hung back, not sure if he was supposed to join this or wait until they were done. Saunders had surely seen him enter, but did not look at him. He was watching Andrews, his sharp face quiet and fierce.

"Sir, the procedure manuals are quite plain in this regard."

Michaels made a chopping motion with his hand.

"Hey, alpha out. I'm telling you, the doc ran off. She did not become bug food."

Andrews spoke with weary and half-angry patience. "Colonel, the Mission Data Packet Transmission is undeniable—"

Michaels interrupted. "Look, I don't know what PacTrans said, but I was there and I'm telling you—Dr. Marks took a walk!"

Saunders continued fingering his beard, and did not look at either of them as he spoke. His face was difficult to read. Was he grieving? Angry? Or simply very abstracted?

"Lieutenant Andrews, how much oxygen did Dr. Marks have remaining at the time of the ambush?"

"PacTrans indicates her O-two supply was at eighty-seven percent."

"How long might a person of Dr. Marks's size survive at eighty-seven percent oxygen?"

"Approximately four and a half hours."

Saunders looked at Andrews. "Begin an immediate search for Dr. Marks within a twelve-mile radius of the crash site."

Andrews shook his head in evident disbelief. "Sir, I must protest. This man is not a reliable source of information."

"Private Michaels' opinions," Saunders put scornful emphasis on the word, "have nothing to do with my decision, Lieutenant. Dr. Marks is critical to the—"

Andrews broke in. "Colonel, we have already lost a skivver to this new bug type. The odds of—"

"Lieutenant," Saunders was clearly angry now. He raised his voice very slightly and coldly overrode the UN man, "according to my calculations, Dr. Marks has only two hours of oxygen remaining. You will commence an immediate search, concluding only with return of the doctor herself or her remains. Am I understood?"

"I would like to protest—"

"Your protests have been duly noted." Saunders snapped. "Put the base on full alert."

"Yes, sir." Andrews glared at Michaels. "Thank you, sir."

Saunders laid his hands flat on his desk. "Dismissed."

Andrews and Michaels turned and walked toward the doors. They kept a careful distance from each other. Michaels saw Griffin, gave him a sardonic grin, and then was gone.

"Private Griffin, might I speak to you for a moment?" Saunders' expression was very quiet. His careful politeness did not make Griffin feel any less uneasy. He walked forward, his shoulders tight with tension. What does *he* want?

"Yes, sir. Certainly, sir."

"Private Griffin . . . You go by Drew, don't you?"

"Yes, sir." He hid his surprise.

"Do you mind if I call you Drew?"

"No, sir. Not at all, sir."

Saunders smiled. He was obviously making an effort to look human. Griffin felt about as reassured as if the lead dog of a feral pack had wagged its tail. He smiled in return.

"Good," said Saunders and smiled. "I have a cousin named Drew." He paused, and Griffin said nothing. "Listen, I know that you and Michaels are friends."

"Yes, sir."

"We are very concerned about Private Michaels' mental state. We have reason to believe he may be unbalanced." Saunders sighed and looked down at his desk. Griffin wished he could read the display he was examining. Unbalanced, eh? What was your first clue? Besides, there's not a single member of Phoenix Company who isn't wonky one way or the other.

For some reason, that thought echoed inside his head like the sound of a big brass gong. He pushed it aside ruthlessly, to think about later.

"There is even some evidence to suggest he may have contributed in some way to the skivver crash."

"Sir," Griffin said, keeping it as flat as possible.

Saunders looked at him. "I want to ask a favor of you."

"Sir?"

"I want you to keep an eye on Private Michaels. If he does or says anything strange—please let me know about it."

Griffin stared, his skin prickling. "Yes, sir." In a pig's eye I will.

"Good. If he does or says anything out of the ordinary, you let me know, won't you?"

Griffin forced himself to nod. He started to move, hoping Saunders would be prompted to dismiss him. No such luck.

"Private, I want to warn you, Dr. Mirren thinks the man may be schizophrenic."

Schizophrenic? Marvelous! Just how stupid do you think I am? A Jensen Ultra would never miss a case of schizophrenia, the brain patterns are too distinctive. Is this a test of some sort? Griffin gazed steadily at Saunders and hoped his face showed nothing.

"I'm inclined to believe he's a subversive. Either way, he may prove to be very dangerous. So I ask you to please be careful."

Griffin felt paralyzed, and couldn't even nod. Saunders sniffed, looked down again, and then smiled tightly at him.

"Drew, thanks very much. I want to thank you for your assistance. We all appreciate it. And it will be reflected on your service record. Dismissed." Saunders spoke almost gently, unlike the curt ejection order he had given Andrews.

Griffin forced himself into motion, fighting hard to resist the urge to run.

Chapter Thirty

Griffin signaled his billet door closed. It was getting to be a habit. The platoon would be gathering by twos and fours right now as the word about Alonzo and Tisch spread. He lay down on his bunk, shoved his hands under his head, and stared at the slowly turning fan in the ceiling. Part of him felt this must be a simulation run, where soon he would take off the TopHat and they'd both be fine, just a bit chastened by being found out.

He felt like his skin was being peeled slowly off him. What was that thought he'd had, staring at the colonel and, behind him, at the deep colors of the stained glass window? Something about the platoon, about—

There isn't a single member of Phoenix Company who isn't wonky one way or the other.

Yeah. That was it. Michaels a troublemaker and

Alonzo and Alvarez not far behind. But Alonzo was dead. Hawkins the defrocked minister. Hotpants Hynick, barely smart enough to control his own hormones and constantly in trouble because of them. Castle the addicted gambler, Lopez's trigger temper, tense Whalen wound as tight as a clock. Tisch, the Green fanatic, the man who knew everything, all the time, about the Earth and her desperate wounds. And Tisch was dead.

And himself, of course. Andrew Griffin, emotional escape artist extraordinaire. Which wouldn't get him automatically stuck in Phoenix Company, but his age would, as would the string of uncompleted dreams and plans and jobs and schooling he trailed after himself.

They had all been astonished when the posting came through, so astonished they hadn't talked about it for fear it would go away. They knew they were the dregs of the division, the platoon where Beatrice kept soldiers it couldn't wash out without breaking contract, but didn't want, or didn't trust, or didn't like. They had expected Rangoon, or even the shambles in Belgium, or to be sent into China when that political bomb finally exploded. They had thought they were considered expendable, until this posting, this hotshot, make-your-career posting. It was their salvation. They were good, they were useful, they were skillful enough to be sent here.

He turned over, wrapping his arms around his

stomach, as he played and replayed the image of the exploding bug. It was so strange. Living things didn't just fall into juiceless pieces—they had blood and guts. But maybe the bugs were a lot more different even than they looked. He'd read speculation about silicon-based life. What if they were structurally more like an evolved robot, with a resemblance to Earth's insects a coincidence of parallel form? Then he shook the speculation away. The important thing was that someone didn't want them to know any more about the bugs, or this planet, and it just didn't make any sense.

What else? No dreams, and his increasing feeling that that was connected to the flashbacks he kept having during the day. A Quantum Gate that its own technician said couldn't work. Free-running water, enough to waste on cleaning yourself. The EEMO forecast. The horrible joy of the sim runs, Dr. Marks vanishing, and a C.O. who wanted him to spy on a friend. Being indentured. And Sergeant Cranshaw holding a cocked pistol under Michaels' chin.

No, Phoenix Company was here for one reason only, and Private Andrew Griffin knew, beyond doubt, what that reason was. They were here because they were expendable. They were here because if they died, nobody would care.

He closed his eyes and discovered he was deeply, terribly, and helplessly angry. He wanted to roar, he wanted to break something, and he was afraid to move for fear he would go completely berserk. He lay there rigid, lost in his internal world of rage.

The anger faded slowly as he breathed, deliberately forcing his muscles to relax. He told himself to stop thinking. He had no answers, and he had no power to do anything even if he'd had answers.

Alonzo and Tisch were dead. Michaels obviously thought their deaths were unnecessary. But what if Andrews was right and the SD devices had saved them from a far more agonizing death?

And what about Saunders? That the man was power hungry and manipulative could be seen from the way he moved. On the other hand, wouldn't anyone in charge of such a major UN project have to be that sort of person?

He remembered the man's face as they spoke. There was something he hadn't quite understood about it. He ran through the images again, horrified.

The man was *frightened*! He was indentured under a scared C.O. Power-hungry and manipulative was bad enough, but fear could impel a man to do nearly anything. As he himself knew, having run from nearly every crisis in his life, to his own lasting shame.

He wished he had some drugs. Alcohol, para-C— anything that would help him stop this useless thinking. He knew deep in his guts that something bad was going on here, something even worse than the obvious, and the obvious was plenty bad enough. And he could do nothing about it. Nothing at all.

Militerm chimed softly and he jumped. A message said that the mess hall had just opened for dinner. He wasn't hungry but he felt deeply and stupidly relieved. At least he had something to do now, something that might occupy his careening mind for a few minutes. He'd get some food and then go to the enlisted lounge. The wake for Alonzo and Tisch would probably be there tonight. Surely someone would come up with some alcohol. He could get blasted and run away and forget all this impossible confusion.

Chapter Thirty-One

The mess hall was deserted. The rows of empty tables in the spare, cold room made him feel like he was the last living person left on the planet. Where was the rest of the platoon? He forced himself forward. They were probably doing more sim runs and would show up soon.

Dinner was as horrible as usual. Examining it provided some distraction. The mess hall AP called it meat loaf. Three gray squares lay unappealingly on his plate. Next to them was a green paste that had been billed as broccoli. Griffin stared at it for a moment, then realized that the veggie machine hadn't been programmed for structure. What did Cookie *do* with his time? He sat down and cut off a chunk of the meat loaf with a fork. It was so dry he immediately took a drink of water. The only taste it had was in the top layer, which crunched and was very salty. Did the veggie machine think he was deficient in sodium?

Dr. Mirren came in while he was carefully chewing the tough food. She seemed subdued. He nodded to her and she set her tray down across from his.

"Hey," he said. "How's Alvarez?"

"Couple of broken ribs." She picked up her cup. "They shipped him earth-side; they'll patch him up there."

Griffin just looked at her. The sick bay was more than adequate for dealing with something simple like a couple of broken ribs.

Mirren saw his expression. "Don't sweat it," she said, and shook her head, shaking away the topic at the same time. "I *hate* doing autopsies," she continued.

Griffin accepted the change in topic. If the military wanted to waste their money shipping busted-up privates around, that was their own business. "Autopsies, huh? That's a great way to start a dinner table conversation."

"Knock it off. You wouldn't have lasted one term at U.T. if you'd been squeamish."

"Well, autopsies beat worrying about whether you're going to cut off the wrong thing and kill a person."

Her grin was a shadow of her usual. "Yeah, I suppose so." She cut off a forkful of meat loaf and put it into her mouth. She didn't even grimace, just chewed carefully. She'd been here longer. Maybe it was possible to get used to this food. "But there's no longer any hope of making things right. You know?"

"Yeah. I know. They just lie there and it's all gone, only the meat left behind."

"Do you believe there's anything else? Something besides the meat?"

Griffin felt wary. "Mostly, I don't. Maybe in a sense, 'cuz our substance gets recycled into new life."

"If there is new life. There might not be."

"You're referring to those EEMO projections?"

"Yes."

"Even if this project doesn't work and life dies, there will be *something* left, won't there? Bacteria or whatever? Give it a little time and things will redevelop."

Mirren nodded. "Very likely. Not a sure thing, but it didn't take Gaia very long to make life the first time and conditions won't be all that much different. Probably won't follow the same path, though."

"Which might not be such a bad thing."

"Too true," she said and ate some more of her meat loaf.

"Mind if I ask you a question?"

She swallowed. "Ask away."

"I can wrap my mind around the idea that we might be close to killing off all human life on Earth.

It's pretty obvious, isn't it? I can even see how we could take it so far that we might kill off most mammals. But virtually all multicellular life? Plants included?"

Dr. Mirren opened her mouth, then closed it. She took another bite of her meat loaf. Griffin's alarm mounted over what she might say the longer she delayed, and he wished he hadn't asked the question.

She put down her fork and looked him in the eyes. For the first time since he'd met her, there was no thought in his mind of her fine body.

"It's a question of balances," she said. "I haven't seen all the data and I'm not qualified to evaluate it anyway. However, it's more than just poisons in the soil and the air. There's a viral mutation that keeps cropping up over and over, one that attacks mitochondria. An even minimally healthy immune system can fight it off. It's probably endemic in many areas. However, as we degrade the health en masse of vast numbers of organisms, this virus spreads. The core virus tends to kill off only those animals and plants that are already pretty much dead. The coup de grace, you might say. But the mutation can gain a foothold in healthy organisms. You remember that nuke along the Ivory Coast two years ago?"

"Sure, who doesn't? The terrorists got careless and—"

"I doubt it. There was a *very* fast wave of death

rolling across that country, taking out everything in its path. Reports stopped coming out after two days and four days after that some terrorists had a nuclear accident."

Griffin felt his face pale. Dr. Mirren nodded. "You see, don't you? What are the odds? And wouldn't you do the same if you had your finger on the button?"

"But they stopped it from spreading, didn't they?"

"Yes. They did. That time. However, the mutation involved is just a chain duplication. It's probably happened a thousand times a decade for millions of years, but never found the right situation waiting for it before. The declining oxygen levels are perfect for it. It's just a matter of time."

Griffin ate in silence for a minute. "So, it takes out everything with mitochondria—essentially the entire Earth—and leaves the world with nothing but slime."

"You got it."

"I hope not."

Dr. Mirren laughed a little too much at his joke. Griffin couldn't laugh at all. As he watched her hair shake in the artificial light, he thought about Phoenix Company again. And about the fact that it's OK to tell secrets to a dying man. Because who is he going to tell?

Chapter Thirty-Two

The mess hall entrance irised open and a chorus of voices tumbled in, followed by what remained of Phoenix Company, with the exception of Private Michaels. Hynick saw Dr. Mirren, colored, then saw Griffin. He elbowed Lopez. The rest of the group noticed, looked over, and fell silent.

After a moment, Castle walked forward and looked Griffin in the eye.

"Is it true?"

Griffin didn't understand her for a second. Is what true? Is the Earth going to die? Is Saunders running scared? Then he realized what she must be saying and sighed. "About Alonzo and Tisch?"

The tall woman nodded. "Yes."

Castle closed her eyes tightly. Whalen and Lopez came up on either side of her. Whalen put a hand gently on her elbow and Castle looked at her.

"Griffin says they're dead," said Castle.

Whalen shuddered, then hugged Castle. Griffin watched, and wondered what he had missed. Which one was Castle grieving? Hynick broke the silence.

"Michaels says there are SD devices on our CO suits."

"I haven't looked for them," said Griffin, "but Andrews didn't deny it."

Hynick looked at Dr. Mirren. "Do you think that's right?"

"That there are SDs on—"

"No, I mean *right*!" Hynick sounded angry. "I mean, should we have self-destruct devices on our suits?"

Dr. Mirren gave him a surprised glance, and Griffin knew she hadn't thought the boy would ever have the nerve to interrupt her. "I can't answer that question. My job is to save lives. That's what I try to do."

"Could you save anyone who'd been exposed to the atmosphere around here?"

"The original UN survey team said it couldn't be done."

"What do *you* think?"

"I . . ." she paused and took a deep breath. "I don't argue with orders."

"Where's Alvarez?" Lopez demanded.

"They shipped him earth-side," Mirren said.

"Did you see them do it?"

Instead of answering, the doctor stood and

picked up her tray. The platoon members watched her dump her tray into the recycler and head for the door.

"Dr. Mirren?" said Castle.

The doctor turned, her face very blank. "Yes?"

"When will you release the bodies for services?"

"I already have. They will be transported back to Earth this evening. The colonel will hold services in the briefing room at twenty-hundred hours. If anyone wishes to view the bodies for a final good-bye, they can go to the Quantum Gate afterward."

"How do they," Castle paused and swallowed hard, "how do they look?"

Dr. Mirren looked puzzled. "Look? They look . . . oh! You're worried that it might be . . . upsetting to see them?"

Castle nodded.

"They look, uh, unhappy. There is nothing worse than that."

"Thank you."

Dr. Mirren nodded to the private and was gone, the door hissing shut behind her.

The rest of the platoon got their dinners. Usually, they spread out through the room in twos and threes, chatting and harassing each other. Tonight, they huddled silently around one table, not even criticizing the food as they ate.

Griffin sat amid them, wondering where Michaels was but afraid to ask.

❖ ❖ ❖

He had worried about whether to wear his dress uniform to the service. There was probably a rule about it somewhere, but he didn't bother to look it up. Tisch and Alonzo deserved what honor he could give them, so he put on the snug-fitting clothes and left the billet.

He wasn't the only one who had made that decision. Whalen, Castle, and Hynick were just ahead of him going into the lift. They nodded, and made room for him as the doors began to close. Castle and Hynick had also chosen the dress uniform. Whalen looked like she was sleepwalking. Griffin glanced at her, saw dilated pupils and realized Dr. Mirren must have given her something.

The rest of the company was already there as they came into the briefing room. Saunders, Andrews, and Cranshaw stood at the front of the room, looking quiet and stern. As Griffin slipped into a seat beside Michaels, he thought the two UN men looked like classic fire-and-brimstone preachers getting set to make their parishioners see the wages of sin. Hell-fire indeed. This planet full of poison and bugs was all the hellfire Griffin or anyone else needed.

Saunders cleared his throat and the room became intensely silent. Even Michaels stilled his usual restless movements.

"We are gathered here to pay our last respects

to two fine young men. I was not privileged to know them personally, but I know their records." He looked slowly around the room, as though challenging them to deny him his right to speak. "They were dedicated and brave soldiers determined to give service back to the world that birthed them, and they paid the highest price any one of us can pay." He paused and looked down, then back at the platoon. "I honor their courage. I ask you to honor it as well by continuing in your fine work on this most important of missions—the task of saving Earth itself. I have sent in my recommendation that both receive the U Thant award for distinguished service in the cause of world peace. Sergeant?"

Cranshaw stood and walked forward. She faced them and planted herself with her hands behind her back. Her face was very white.

"You are one of the finest platoons I've had the privilege to lead. We will miss our comrades deeply. Alonzo was a talented pilot and his sharp sense of humor helped us past many rough spots. Tisch had a knack for knowing when someone needed a helping hand. They were assets to all of us, both as a platoon and as human beings."

She was silent a moment. Griffin's throat felt tight. He heard someone sniff and glanced over to see tears running down Castle's face. To his surprise, Michaels also had a shiny streak on his cheek and Hawkins was crying even more openly than Castle.

"Does anyone wish to speak a few words before we proceed to the Gate?"

Whalen rose. Her voice shook and squeaked. Griffin could barely hear what she said. Something about Alonzo but more about Tisch. Michaels rose and told a somewhat cleaned-up version of the time they had all been hauled up for curfew violations. Hawkins spoke of meeting Alonzo's family. Castle talked about the time Tisch had beaten her at skyball.

Griffin tried to think of something he could say, but nothing came to mind. He kept thinking of his father's funeral, with his mother's stream of tears and his sister cold as ice. The services had been Gaia, and he'd been angry at his mother for that. Still, he knew that even though his father was not of that faith, Dad would not have objected to Mom choosing whatever service would comfort her most.

A few minutes of silence passed. Cranshaw looked at Saunders, who nodded.

"Transport to Earth will commence in fifteen minutes. Anyone wishing to pay final respects or to be present at transport may come with us now."

Saunders and Andrews led the way, with Cranshaw following close behind. The platoon rose as one, and filed out. Whalen silently turned into the hallway toward the lift as they passed. Hynick followed her. The rest of the platoon continued on toward the Quantum Gate. Griffin hesitated outside the door. It closed behind Michaels and he was left alone in the corridor. You'll stop dreaming. No more dreams for Alonzo and Tisch. In med school someone had said that three days without REM sleep was sufficient to induce psychosis in most humans. How could they do without dreams?

Griffin shook himself as he heard the Gate start to hum from the other side of the door. He walked toward it, the door opened, and he entered. Two figures lay on the platform. Alonzo's face was contorted, the dark skin twisted as though he might shout at any second. Tisch looked vastly and terribly surprised. The huge crystal flower-petals of the Gate rose around them as the Gate's roar intensified. Bubbles of light streamed toward the triangle set into the ceiling.

Less than a minute later, it was over. The oblong crystals opened and the bodies were gone. Griffin blinked, his vision clouded with after images of the glowing lights. Charlie Becker stood against a far wall, fiddling with a bank of controls. Becker claimed that he didn't understand how the Gate could transport anything, but it clearly did.

Griffin thought about the men appearing back on Earth, maybe in the same hangar they'd left such a short time ago. He remembered their faces. He started to walk out, stopped in midstep, and Hynick ran into him. The kid mumbled an apology, then continued on as Griffin looked at the Gate's platform again. Sarge said that the atmosphere of AJ3905 could eat your face. Andrews said the SDs prevented a painful death. The SDs were only activated when you were exposed to the outside air. A chemical stew that could eat your face would do it whether you were alive or not. Why had Tisch and Alonzo looked OK?

Chapter Thirty-Three

The entire platoon except for Whalen was in the enlisted lounge. Sarge produced the first bottle. To Griffin's surprise, Hawkins produced a second. No one was surprised when Michaels left briefly and returned with two more.

They tried to do the wake right. They told stories from the old days and played a little skyball and drank heavily. Yet none of them seemed really able to let go. Griffin wondered if they all felt the way he did, so dazed by events that alcohol made no real difference.

Cranshaw left comparatively early, and they all knew she was releasing them to let down their hair without the sarge around. They protested in a formal way, telling her to stay, but she didn't. After the door closed behind her, there was a short silence. They were clustered around several tables pulled together.

"OK, Michaels—give," said Hawkins.

Michaels folded his arms. "What you talking about?"

"Tell us what happened."

Michaels just looked at him.

"Michaels, we need to know. We deserve to," said Castle.

Michaels put his face into his hands. Griffin watched him, puzzled. What's he doing? Michaels doesn't cover his face, he puts it in yours.

Michaels leaned back, looking distant. "Dr. Marks called in our team. She was cheerful as hell but didn't tell us what we were going to do. She just gave Tisch the coordinates and we headed out. She had me, Alonzo, and Alvarez sitting around watching a clip of some geological formation. I don't know what *that* was about.

"I was nearly freaking asleep when Tisch started yelling about flying bugs. Then we got tossed around a lot. Alvarez was on weapons. I heard him start firing, but he stopped suddenly. You'll have to ask him why."

Griffin made a noise, and Michaels looked at him, first in annoyance, then his expression grew very still.

"What?" he demanded.

"They shipped Alvarez earth-side, after we got back. He's not here anymore." Griffin said it for them all to hear, but he kept his eyes on Michaels' face. "He's not here to ask anymore."

Michaels was still for a moment, then for another moment his lips formed soundless curses. He stopped abruptly and put his shoulders back, pushing it all away.

"OK. That's something for later." He breathed deeply. "We went down. It was pretty harsh. One pontoon ripped loose, and Alvarez got knocked out. Then we were stopped."

He paused to take a deep breath. Nobody said anything.

"The doc, she didn't seem upset," he continued. "She jumped into her envirosuit, slapped her helmet on, and was cycling out through the airlock before any of us knew what was happening."

"She jumped out into a mess of bugs?" said Hynick.

"Listen—I don't know *what* she ran into. I wasn't anywhere near a screen. I just know she was gone." Michaels looked around, as though daring them to believe it. No one spoke.

"So there was something wrong with Alvarez, he was still down. But his suit was OK. Understand?"

He waited, staring at them, until one by one they nodded.

"OK," he said. "Tisch said I should cover them on weapons while he and Alonzo went out to help the Doc. Made sense to me at the time."

Michaels stopped and stared up, his face very still. The moment stretched on a long time. They could all see him reliving the crash.

"Come on, guy," said Hynick softly.

"Yeah, yeah, don't short-circuit," Castle said.

Michaels shook himself and looked back at the waiting platoon. "Tisch and Alonzo cycled out. Alvarez was groaning on the floor. I stepped over him and got on the weapons. The screens were all jazzed, I couldn't see much. Flashes of wacky stuff, green stuff, then bugs, then green stuff, then nothing. I could hear Tisch or Alonzo firing, Alonzo started yelling, I got a clear sight long enough to nail one bug, and then it was all quiet. Too quiet. I couldn't raise Tisch, Alonzo, or Dr. Marks. The ship's AP was flashing in and out of existence, but told me that the SD units on Tisch and Alonzo had activated. That was the first time I heard about them. I tried to get the skivver up, but it wasn't moving. So I called for an assist and slapped a medipatch on Alvarez."

There was a long silence, then Hawkins spoke abruptly, "You didn't go out and try to help Tisch and Alonzo?" His face was accusing and his hands formed fists.

Michaels stared at him silently for a heartbeat. "Man, did you hear me? They were *dead*!" His voice rose to a near shout. "You *know* they were dead. The SD units activated on both, and made sure they died." Michaels leaned forward in his chair, his hands flattened to the table. He started to stand up.

Hawkins glared back at him.

"Michaels, power down." said Castle, her tough face disgusted. "Hawkins, you're going too far."

Hawkins looked at her, his face a study in mixed emotions. Then he nodded tightly. He looked at Michaels. "You're right. Sorry, guy."

Michaels blinked rapidly and relaxed. "Unlock and unload. We're all freaking out around this stuff."

"No joke," said Castle. "I'm going to be running replays of this in my dreams."

"Don't count on it," said Michaels. Castle looked puzzled, but he went on talking as though she hadn't reacted. "I could swear Marks knew something was going to happen. I don't know what, but this whole business is clogging my tubes."

"How did the bugs get past the detectors?" said Lopez.

"Good question. You answer that and I'll be a happy grunt."

"Don't count on it," Castle said, but nobody laughed.

Chapter Thirty-Four

Griffin had pulled off his dress uniform and slid into a more comfortable set of khakis when the door chimed.

A minute later, Michaels sauntered in, thumbs hooked on the belt of his fatigue pants.

"Hey, man—how ya doing?"

Griffin looked at him tiredly.

"I've been better, actually," he said.

"Yeah, me too. Hey, what's Saunders want with you?"

Griffin shook his head. "You'll like this. He wanted me to keep an eye on you and report back with anything funny."

"Krishna on a Christmas tree, that's typical. Saunders! What a brownie hound. So, what'd ya tell him?"

"Hell, what do you think? I didn't tell him anything."

Michaels nodded, but Griffin wasn't sure he

believed him.

"Listen, I need to talk to you about something."

"Yeah? Well listen here, I need to talk to you more. Sit down."

Michaels looked surprised, but sat on the bunk. Griffin scooted the chair close.

"OK, I've been doing some thinking. Don't make any smart-ass remarks, Michaels." Leaning forward, he laid it on the line, everything he had learned that didn't make sense to him, and everything he conjectured. Michaels listened in silence, his eyes never moving from Griffin's face.

When Griffin finally sat back he felt drained, as though he had lanced something and let all the pressure out. Michaels raised his eyebrows.

"I knew there was a reason I was wasting my time with you," he said, and for the first time in days he gave Griffin a real smile, one that lit up the hard planes of his face. "That business about getting the nurse to scan the flower, that's pretty good."

"Well, gee, thanks," Griffin retorted. "At least it's trying to get some kind of proof. Because without that, we've got squat, Michaels, and you know it."

"Maybe. Maybe not." Michaels was silent for a moment. "When you were flying out there to get us, you got attacked right? By one of the flying things?"

"Yeah, so?"

"OK, bear with me. When you fly, you're using

a TopHat. We used those same kinda TopHats in Belgium."

He paused. This time Griffin just watched him, and finally Michaels said, "We thought we were going in to take out a bunker of Common Soil snipers. And I got this weird feeling one time, y'know, just this thought, so I took off my TopHat." He stopped and took a deep breath. His voice dropped to a whisper. "Do you remember the assassination of the Transprogressionist Party president and his family?"

"Yes."

"Remember that picture, the little girl holding her doll, just kinda lying there?"

Griffin remembered the picture. Perhaps the most powerful propaganda item ever used against Common Soil, it showed the president's five-year-old daughter clutching her doll—except that the doll's head, and the little girl's chest, had been blown away.

"I saw it happen, man," Michaels said so softly Griffin had to lean forward to catch his words. "It wasn't Common Soil that did it."

Griffin stared, and Michaels nodded once.

"OK," he continued, his voice almost normal but still low. "On patrol today, three things. The good doctor did *not* eat it in a bug fight. She was ten klicks off the flight path, she knew what she was doing and I'm telling ya, man, she *walked* away. Now, somebody altered the PacTrans data. My guess is it was Andrews. I just can't figure out why."

Griffin nodded. "You want me to believe that Dr. Marks deliberately walked away, into an atmosphere that can kill you. Walked away from her work, from her family, all that stuff? Jeez, Michaels."

"Griffie, please, just gimme a chance here."

"OK," Griffin said finally. "For argument's sake, I'll buy it."

Michaels nodded. "The second thing. After we were down, after I took over the bubble. The screens, the VR display in there, it kept doing some strange shit, man. I mean, it's like I'd be seeing brown hills, all that ugly shit out there, and then— I don't know, man." He shook his head. "It was like someone had programmed in a picture, you know? A real old one, with blue sky, and trees—green stuff, like a painting—but just a flash, and then it'd be gone again."

Griffin wet his lips. "Yeah," he said. But the growing cold in his stomach didn't let him say any more.

"And the third thing," Michaels continued. "Just before his suit was breached, Alonzo was screaming for us not to shoot, he was saying, 'They're human! Don't fire! They're people.'"

Griffin's guts hurt, that I-gotta-get-outa-here ache that he knew so well, and he started to lose his temper. "Then why didn't you report it?" he demanded.

"Are you really that stupid? If it's true, do you

think Saunders doesn't know it? He'd just give me crap about VR addressing errors. But you know what really cuts it, Griffie? It had to be on the PacTrans, because that sucker records everything. And they're claiming it's not there." His eyes narrowed. "I'm telling ya, man, the VR is *not* accurate, and they're lying about the PacTrans, and they lied to us about the SD units, too."

"They didn't lie," Griffin said. "They just didn't tell us."

"It's called a sin of omission," Michaels said. "Do you realize what they are doing with those SD units on our suits?" He didn't give Griffin a chance to answer. "They say it's to protect us from a protracted and painful death on the surface of AJ3905, they have rigged out envirosuits with self-destruct modules. What triggers this wonderfully humane action? Any breach of the suit, right? Including voluntarily taking off the helmet."

Even a voluntary suit breach would trigger the SD? "Wait a minute, why would anyone want to take off a TopHat?"

"I asked myself the same question in Belgium. And listen—if they are not giving us a VR compatibility drug, then why was it I was able to find an antidote?" Michaels held up a foiled packet containing three white pills, and looked at it smugly.

"Where did you—no," Griffins said, interrupting himself. "I don't want to know."

Michaels put the pills on the table. The two men stared at them.

"Another station?" Griffin said after a long time.

"No way of knowing."

"One mechanic?"

"Don't know why."

"Gate tech can't figure out why the Gate works."

Michaels shrugged. "Can't answer that one, either. Maybe he's asking the wrong questions, or expecting it to do something it's not designed to do." And Griffin remembered Charlie Becker saying that they were not, necessarily, on AJ3905. Trinidad, the crazy little tech had muttered. Or Sumatra.

"Strange plant life," Michaels said.

"Don't know, man."

"Sunlight."

"Maybe, maybe not."

Michaels paused, then said, "You know Charlie Becker? That wimp Gate tech?"

Griffin nodded.

"I talked to him tonight. He says the Gate was only used once today. To transport Tisch and Alonzo."

Griffin stared at him blankly for a moment, then it hit him.

"Then where's Alvarez?" he said.

"Where do you think?" Michaels slammed both palms against the table. "There's one person on board who knows the answers, and who has to tell us."

"Yeah?" Griffin said. "What you gonna do, ask Saunders?"

"No," Michaels said, standing. "No, I'm coming back for you around oh-three-hundred hours. Central Processing's deserted then." He looked down at Griffin. "Under the International Information Act you have a right to access your personnel file at any time." He paused. "So we're going to have a little talk with The Beast."

Chapter Thirty-Five

Griffin was desperately tired when Michaels left. Soul deep weary. He stripped to his underwear and didn't even bother putting the clothes into the recycler. Leaving them in an untidy heap on the floor, he crawled into his bunk and closed his eyes. The dark tide of sleep swept him under.

"Hey, Griffie." A voice in his room. Not the AP's wake up call. Who? Griffin sat up. Michaels was standing over him with a hand on his shoulder. "Come on," he said. "Wake up. Time to go."

Griffin stood, and pulled on his fatigue pants. He felt like he had just closed his eyes. How could it be oh-three-hundred already? Michaels headed out. Griffin followed. The lift sounded impossibly loud in the quiet of the night and their footsteps seemed to echo. He expected a guard around every bend and jumped when a ventilator clanked as he was going by. However, they didn't see a single human being during their short walk to the computer center.

The computer's AI greeted them as they walked in the door, its huge and inhuman face hanging in the air before them. "Hello, Privates Michaels and Griffin. How may I assist you?"

Griffin stopped in his tracks, staring up and feeling like it could read his every thought. Some people said a true AI could do the next best thing. With the right sensory gear, they could detect extremely minute changes in body temperature and scent. With that face looking down on him, he found stories that he had previously dismissed as paranoid a lot more plausible. What was he doing here?

Michaels said, "Ask for access to your personnel file."

Griffin looked at him, looked back at the AI, and squeaked out, "Uh, may I have access to my personal records?" He swallowed. "Please."

Michaels gave him a disgusted look. The AI didn't bother to answer. It rotated its bodiless face toward a display screen on Griffin's left, and his records began to scroll by.

"Medical record," said Michaels briskly. "Search medications, please." The record display blurred, then paused. "Read line three."

"Three hundred cc Myadonna nitrate, delivered daily," said the AI.

"Close file. Open my personnel file, please. Search medications." Michaels scanned the display briefly, then said, "Read line five."

"Three hundred cc Myadonna nitrate, delivered daily."

Michaels looked out from under his eyebrows at Griffin. "You taking any medication?"

"No."

"Me, neither." He signaled the computer to close the files. "With that high a quantity, they're probably delivering it in the water supply." He turned toward the AI. "Is that true? Is my Myadonna medication being delivered in the water supply?"

"Negative," said the AI, and Griffin could have sworn that it sounded amused.

"Is Myadonna delivered to everyone on this station?" Griffin asked.

"That is not a pertinent question," the AI said.

Michaels faced the Face. "OK. How about this? What is the Myadonna prescribed for?"

"Sleep disorders," the AI said.

"Are there any indications, in my record, of sleep disorders?" Michaels said.

"There are indications going back three months."

"That's bullshit! I've *never* had problems—"

"Who entered that information into the record?" Griffin said.

"Access denied."

Griffin took a deep breath. "OK. Who entered

that information into *my* record?"

"Access denied."

Michaels looked like he was about to shout, but Griffin put a hand on his shoulder. "Wait, think it through. If you're right, then—" He turned to the AI. "Does Myadonna disrupt REM sleep?"

"Affirmative," the AI said.

"Is Myadonna shown to enhance VR compatibility?"

"Affirmative."

"Who else is getting it, then?" Michaels demanded.

"Access denied." Griffin could have sworn that the AI sounded smug.

"Wait, wait," Griffin said. "On this station, how are medications administered?"

"Access denied."

"OK. How are *my* medications administered?"

"Orally," the AI said promptly.

"Great," Griffin said with satisfaction. "And it's not in the water, so it has to be in the food. And the mess hall AP identifies each of us when we order, and the veggie machine is programmed to supply each dose. Am I correct?"

"You are correct."

Griffin grinned. "About Myadonna's side effects. Does the drug taste bad?"

"It is so described," the AI said.

"Aha. And is its active ingredient formulated with something that dulls the taste buds?"

There was a moment of silence, then the AI said, "Affirmative."

Griffin's grin spread. "Michaels," he said. "I think we owe Cookie an apology."

Michaels didn't find it amusing. "The hell we do." He narrowed his eyes, then said, "OK, let's try this one. Why is there only one mechanic at this station?"

"That is not pertinent to your private personnel file," the AI said tolerantly. "Access denied."

"I'm a pilot," Griffin said. "It's pertinent if I have to go up in a skivver that isn't adequately maintained. So why is there only one mechanic?"

"Access denied," the AI repeated. "If and when you go up in an inadequately maintained skivver, and if and when a problem arises therefrom, then the information will be pertinent to your file."

Griffin took a deep, frustrated breath and was about to let it out when Michaels said quickly, "Where's Private Alvarez?"

The silence stretched for a moment, then the AI said, "Access denied."

"Was he shipped back to Earth?" Michaels persisted.

"Access denied."

"Is he still on this planet?" Griffin demanded.

"Access denied."

"Is he in sick bay?" Michaels pressed.

"Access denied."

"Is he alive?" Griffin asked.

And, once again, the AI skipped a beat, barely perceptible unless you were listening for it, unless you knew that AIs never, never needed time to think, to formulate a response. And, once again, the AI said, "Access denied."

Michaels cursed violently, but Griffin simply stood, looking at the green face of the AI. It looked back at him, without expression. The world seemed, quite suddenly, like an insubstantial place.

Is he alive?

The AI had let a moment pass, a bare nanosecond.

Access denied.

The session went rapidly downhill, almost as if the AI had grown bored with their questions and just wanted them to go away. Griffin shook away his momentary feeling of unease. He and Michaels asked about the Gate, about the green visions both had seen in the bubble's VR screens, about the PacTrans record, about Alonzo's astonishing words spoken before he died. The AI denied access, refused pertinence, and responded with flat, endless, and negative politeness to anything they asked that did not show up in their personnel files. Finally Michaels spread his arms in frustrated resignation, and walked away. Griffin watched him go.

He had long ago lost any sense of amusement or adventure, and he felt alone and under observation, standing in the quiet of the computer center after the door closed. The AI's face still hung in the air, but did not seem to be active. What did it make of this? Part of him wanted to ask, to explore the obvious intelligence behind that quiescent green face, to see if it would give him answers.

But a larger part of him shivered and quailed and didn't want to know *anything*. He was afraid. Terribly, primevally afraid—of the AI, of the mission, of Michaels, even of himself. He was a private in the Beatrice Military Division. He was indentured. They could kill him, legally, for no reason at all.

He backed out, and the eyes of The Beast never moved. He dripped sweat as he took the lift back down. Too much was happening. Mysterious gadgets and bugs and platoon members dying and a C.O. pushing at him and thoughts of Jenny haunting him all the way through it. And where was Alvarez? He felt as if he was about to lose it, just crack apart and never hold his head up again.

Michaels' door was tightly closed as he walked past toward his own room. He closed his own door, then grimly put himself through a series of exercises that at least changed the odor of his sweat. When the trembling in his body changed from fear to exhaustion, he took a shower. For the first time, he didn't question the water flowing over his back or feel guilty about it, he just enjoyed it.

The narrow bed called to him as he came out,

still slightly damp from the hot-air dryer. He crawled in and was asleep before he had a chance to ask himself if he would be able to.

Chapter Thirty-Six

S arge was standing over him. "Private Griffin. Griffin!" She clapped her hands twice. He grunted. "Wake up solider, you're needed in the briefing room immediately." She started to walk away and his eyes started to drift closed. She turned, saw him, walked back, and pointed into his face. "Don't go back to sleep."

"Yes, Sergeant."

"Good. Get down there as soon as you can."

Only Hawkins was missing when he arrived in the briefing room. Andrews, Cranshaw, and Saunders stood at the front of the room, looking at the platoon as they settled themselves. The UN men were in their full-bore monkey suits again. Griffin sat next to Michaels, as usual, but didn't look at him. No one was talking, not even to complain about getting rousted early for a briefing. Maybe they were all as dazed as he was. Hawkins came less than a minute later.

Lieutenant Andrews stepped forward. "Can I have your attention please?" He turned to his left. "Colonel Saunders."

Saunders stepped forward. His face was tight. Griffin wasn't sure if he was imagining it, but he thought the edge of fear was stronger today. "Yesterday a survey flight led by Dr. Marks was attacked."

Drew heard an odd catch in Saunders' voice, a not quite stop before he said the last word. A lie. Saunders had just lied.

"There have been two fatalities." said Saunders. "Dr. Marks is missing. Computer model display please."

So they still hadn't found her body. How could they miss it? She'd been wearing a CO suit and a UN uniform, both of which contained materials that ought to be detectable at a distance. Even if she had been ripped out of both by the bugs, wouldn't they have found some traces?

An AP appeared and said, "Playback ready."

The screen filled with an image of a winged bug. In general shape, it looked much like what Griffin had seen yesterday. Gray body, green spiky wings twice its height, two arms, three legs, and a face like an angry dragonfly.

Drew frowned. It seemed to him that this bug had a lot more detail than yesterday's. Was that just because the attack happened so fast? There had also been something else just as that thing blew up. A flash of white, a song from childhood . . . he couldn't quite bring it to mind.

"We have a new bug type," said Saunders. "This is a ComSen report from the VR mission recorders. This new class is considered very dangerous. The added mobility is obviously a factor as well. The VR DB has been updated with this new model so your heads up displays will reflect the proper image. These new bugs have been rated 89A for combat efficiency."

Griffin blinked. *That* news cleared the fog in his head, at least for the moment. 89A?! I'm only a 92 in full armor. We were damn lucky to nail that thing yesterday!

"New directives from ComSen state, 'No skivver deployment when bug type F-1 combatants are present.'"

Huh? What were they going to do? Send grunts out on foot after bugs that could fly? That made no sense. Was it because of that skivver losing pillow?

"And finally, there have been some reports of VR displays malfunctioning. It seems some bugs are being shown as humanoid."

Michaels made a sharp but quickly halted movement. Griffin felt the blood drain out of his face. Last night, Michaels had claimed that Alonzo saw the bugs as human. Display malfunctions. He'd seen some on his own flight. Not Bugs as humans, but the gray and brown landscape suddenly flickered into green, almost as though there was normal vegetation down there.

"So, everyone, please review your on-line manuals on envirosuit procedures and VR error addressing. That, ladies and gentlemen, will be all."

Saunders stared coldly at Griffin.

"Private Griffin. Will you please be so kind as to join me in my quarters at ten-hundred hours?"

Griffin nodded uncomfortably and Saunders left. Did the C.O. expect a report on Michaels' subversive activities? Griffin looked at Michaels, who raised one eyebrow sardonically. Lieutenant Andrews motioned to Cranshaw who stood and faced them.

"OK, folks—new sim runs today. You've been so gung-ho that I put in for more bays yesterday. They came in overnight. We don't have to split up anymore. This is critical stuff, so we'll start right after breakfast."

Hynick groaned, as did Castle.

"Button it." Cranshaw didn't crack a smile. "I'm not planning on losing any more of you. You get in here at oh-seven-hundred and you *work*."

She was angry. Not at them, near as Griffin could tell as they filed out. Just angry.

As he waited in line for his turn at the mess hall AP, his stomach churned. What did Saunders want this time? Judging by his C.O.'s face, he was in trouble. The only question was, what kind and how much?

"What makes those new bugs so blasted tough? 89A!" said Castle, and shook her head. "Sure, they can fly—but the Ortho type can hop so high they might as well be flyers, and no one's ranking them like that."

"Ever heard of an Ortho making a skivver lose pillow?" said Michaels.

The table went silent for a moment. Griffin ate another piece of his flattened waffle. His mind was still moving like mud. Flying bugs. Detailed wings. Myadonna. Alvarez.

He heard the mess hall door open behind him but didn't look up. Hawkins was facing the door.

"John! Hey, come on over here. Got a question for you," said Hawkins. Griffin turned to see the smiling mechanic approaching.

"Sure thing. What can I do for you?"

"How'd that bug make a skivver lose pillow?"

John DiSilva's smile dimmed only slightly. "Don't know. They haven't given me the wreck yet."

"Any guesses?"

"Well, a laser cannon to the outrigger might do it."

"Get serious. The bugs don't have more weapons than what they were born with."

"Sure, sure. But like I said, I just don't know."

DiSilva smiled again, and went to get his food. Hawkins made room for him at the table.

"You must be pleased that we won't be using the skivvers for a while," said Michaels.

DiSilva shrugged. "Don't make no never mind to me."

"But you have to maintain them. If we aren't going out then you've got less work."

The mechanic laughed. "Oh, those babies are easy. No problem at all."

"Don't you have problems with corrosion?

"Corrosion? Naw, naw—no problem at all."

"But the atmosphere has a lot of chlorine. That ought to eat things good," said Hawkins.

DiSilva shrugged again. "Search me. Those babies come back *clean*. Haven't had to replace so much as a single fitting."

"Maybe that's because we aren't on an alien planet," said Michaels. "We're on Earth and they're lying to us for some reason."

The rest of the platoon tensed, but DiSilva didn't seem to notice. He stared at Michaels, then shook his head. "Boy, you been talking to Charlie too much."

"Charlie knows the Gate, and he says some strange things."

"He purely does, doesn't he? Maybe he's even right once in a while. But I tell you, we are *not* on Earth."

"How do you know?"

"I already told you. No corrosion. Does that sound like Earth to you?" He laughed.

Griffin blinked, and then he got it. Respiratory problems were one of the most common ailments in the world, just below water deprivation. Jenny had lost a patient to hyperpneumonia her first time on ER duty. She'd cried in his arms that night, describing the young woman gasping and bubbling out her last breaths. Jenny in his arms. Jenny.

"Maybe the skivvers have just got some good material coatings?" said Michaels.

"And I wouldn't know a coating if I saw one?" DiSilva laughed again. "Listen, boy—maybe I ain't the highest power laser in the army but I *do* know my skivvers. You rest yourself about that stuff. We'd have more trouble with pitting if we were in Antarctica. We are *not* on Earth."

They finished their breakfasts in almost complete silence.

Chapter Thirty-Seven

Sarge had implied she was going to run them ragged in sim, and she was true to her word. Like always. From the time Griffin pulled on his TopHat until she gave them a break an hour later, the onslaught of simulated bugs was relentless. She wouldn't even let folks back out when they got killed, but instead required they continue watching the current scenario play out.

"Just 'cuz you messed up, you think that means you don't have anything more to learn? Try that on your mother." Her anger was colder now, more focused, but still intense. Did she know something they didn't?

Griffin's head felt more clear with nearly every run. He got nailed over and over in the first two runs, as did most of the platoon, but by the third run they were reacting faster.

Sarge's voice came over the TopHat's com line. "OK, crew—now that you're waking up we're going to get tactical for a while."

The bugs began with a diversionary side attack followed by a full assault in formation. The first time the entire platoon was wiped out. Griffin was stunned. *This* is why they got ranked 89A. Was this based on actual observations? If so, someone had known about those flying bugs a lot longer than they were admitting. Yet, if this attack style wasn't real, why would they bother with it under sim?

After that fiasco, the platoon began to sharpen up. Griffin was finally able to nail a few bugs of his own. God, it was good to see those things blow up! He heard Hynick whoop repeatedly. Michaels didn't say a word.

"OK, folks," said Sarge. "Take a rest."

The sim universe went dark and Griffin's TopHat lifted off. He almost pulled it back down over his head and went at it again. He felt great. He didn't need a rest. He could do this all day long. He heard Castle grumble at Sarge, and figured she must feel the same way.

But Sarge was powering down the equipment, looking more satisfied but still too grim to challenge, even as a joke.

Most of the platoon headed for the enlisted lounge. Castle tried to interest some of them in a game of poker, but she'd been winning too heavily lately. No one bit. Hawkins challenged her to sky-ball. She shrugged and accepted.

Whalen and Griffin went back to quarters. He saw Captain Zhorchow's back retreating down the corridor as they came out of the lift. What a relief—he'd missed him! As Whalen signaled her door open, Griffin nodded to her but she either didn't notice or didn't feel like responding. He couldn't recall having heard her speak a word all day. The shock of losing her family had hit deep.

The door to his room closed behind him and the euphoria from sim began to slip away. He sat in his chair, watching the feeling fade and realizing it was like coming down from a rec drug. He could almost see his mood change minute by minute.

And then suddenly he knew.

The TopHats were a substitute for REM sleep. Humans had to have dreams, whether they remembered them or not. His dreams had been getting more thin and scattered ever since arriving on the base. The last two times he'd slept he hadn't had any dreams.

All VR-enhancing drugs repressed REM sleep, which was why they were so seldomly used. The hotshots must have figured out how to get the TopHats to compensate for that. He could almost see how it might be done.

He took the packet of pills from the counter in the bathroom and looked at them. An antidote. Did he believe that? He turned it in his hands. No labeling, not even code numbers. It could be anything.

Sinus medicine, tranquilizer, speed. Yet he knew the shapes and colors of most common medicines. This wasn't quite like any of them.

He set the packet down. Yes, he did believe Michaels. At least that far. He tapped Militerm for intrabase communication and called the lounge. Hynick said Michaels wasn't there. He tried his room, but got no answer.

Probably wandering around, seeing if he could get into more trouble.

What if Michaels was also right about the accuracy of the VR? What did that mean? He claimed Alonzo said they were shooting at humans. Yet DiSilva was dead certain they weren't on Earth and he'd made a good case for it. Let's say the images are doctored to make us happier about killing them. The locals are cute little bunnies instead of ugly bugs.

That still didn't explain a mining operation with no miners, just soldiers. Pacifying the archipelago so the miners wouldn't get attacked? If so, it wasn't working very well, was it? The bugs, or whatever they were, had gotten tougher.

Marks was gone. Probably dead, but Michaels didn't seem to think so. The Gate. The fear in Saunders' eyes. Alvarez. Access denied.

They all roiled around in his brain and, for the first time in his life, Drew Griffin began to think about not running away.

Chapter Thirty-Eight

As he turned to the door, Militerm spoke. "Mail is waiting for you."

He froze. Jenny. It had to be Jenny. He hesitated for only a second before sliding into the chair in front of the terminal. He took a deep breath, not knowing whether he felt fear, or anticipation, but knowing only that, one way or another, this had to be resolved. Then he tapped the screen for the letter.

Words scrolled up the screen:

NOTICE: The following correspondence has been digitally obscured at the request of the sender.

The notice faded and was replaced by Jenny's face. Or rather, half of her face. The right side was heavily blurred. He couldn't quite see what was wrong, but it seemed obvious that her eye at least wasn't right.

"Hi, Drew. How are you? I hope that you are doing well. I'm doing good. We're all . . . good here."

She hesitated. "I . . . I miss you. I, um, I'm worried about you. I hope that you are . . . OK. They won't tell us *anything*, y'know. Where you are. My therapist, Barbara, says that it's either Chile or Budapest. I try not to think about it very much." She gave a short laugh. "But I'm not having very much luck." She was starting to cry. "I . . . you're on my mind all the time, as a matter of fact. Bet you don't have that problem."

He touched the screen, touched the image of her bright hair. Oh, Jenny. My brave, sweet Jenny.

"I still don't know what happened to me. I don't know what happened to . . . us." She closed her eyes briefly and visibly forced herself to calm down. She looked out from the screen with an intent expression. "I want you to know that I don't blame you. And I wish that you don't blame yourself. Y'know, sometimes it just happens.

"Your mom is *really* worried. But I'm doing my best to make her feel better. I know that . . . we can never be together . . . after . . . this. But that doesn't mean you can't come back and pick things up again. And I'm not saying that for you. I'm saying that for your Mom and for me. It would help me a lot if you would . . . come back home. And start school again."

He leaned forward, watching her dear and serious face.

"I'm going to. In a, a year or so," she said.

She didn't sound like even she believed that. He

doubted that his mother did.

"So, who knows? Maybe I'll run into you on campus."

Each word sent shock waves through him. She was so wounded, her body so broken, and yet this was still Jenny. He remembered her spirit, her determination, and wondered if maybe she might really be able to do it.

"I . . . I love you. I love you very much and I'm gonna miss you. Good-bye, Drew."

She turned her head toward someone off camera and Griffin saw where her right eye had been. An enormous thick scar covered the entire area. A failed attempt to regrow the orb. Oh, Jenny. Sweet Jenny.

"Could you turn off the tape?" she said. "I'm finished."

The screen went blank.

Tears streamed down his face and he finally realized that he was going back to her. No matter what it took, he needed, finally, to go back, to stop running. To face his own life.

He said as much, immediately, into Militerm's mail reply module, letting the tears shine on his face, begging her to take him back, to wait for him until his enlistment term was up. And, finally, begging her to forgive him, as he had never, in his life, asked for forgiveness before.

Jenny had a sense of ethics. She puzzled out what

'she felt was right, and then she kept to it. His mother was the same way. They weren't responsibilities to be run from, he thought. They were role models. To hold on to what you believe is right, to fight for it, was the only right way to live.

Andrew Griffin, finally, took control of his own soul.

Chapter Thirty-Nine

Griffin palmed his door closed and stood for a moment, staring at the doors of the other platoon members. Where to start? Michaels still wasn't responding to a page, and, with Alonzo gone, Griffin didn't quite know who to trust—at least, not yet.

Charlie Becker had told Michaels that the Gate had only been used once yesterday, to transport the bodies of Alonzo and Tisch back to Earth. Dr. Mirren had said Alvarez was shipped home. Deep in thought, Griffin strode into the main corridor and almost collided with Marie Lukas. They both stared at each other, shocked.

"Good Lord!" the nurse said. "I tell you, I hadn't realized how much I'd gotten used to it being empty around here." She offered him a smile. "You damn near scared me ragged, soldier. You owe me a stiff cup of tea."

Before he could respond, she took his arm and

steered him toward the enlisted lounge.

"Better hot water in here," she said, and laughed as though she had made a joke. Griffin didn't get it, until they entered the room. A skyball game was in progress, four soldiers from Phoenix Company against some UN guards, and the room almost bounced with noise. The perfect cover for a quiet conversation, he realized as Marie Lukas picked out a table not too far from the game. She kept up a constant chatter about inconsequentialities. She made him get her a cup of tea from the AP, and when he put it down, she reached into her uniform pocket.

"I carry my own sugar," she said. "Use up a lot of my mass allowance on it, but you can't beat the real thing, can you? Here, have some." She grabbed his hand and pressed a neat fold of paper into his palm. Griffin stared at it for a moment, then smiled, and thanked her, and pretended to open up the packet and pour something into his tea. Then, letting his hand fall into his lap, he tucked the piece of paper into his own pocket.

When he looked up again, Marie was regarding him seriously.

"You got my life there, soldier boy," she said without a trace of humor. "Don't you go getting me killed."

He covered her hand with his and squeezed, then drank off part of his tea.

"One more thing," he said, and smiled as inanely as he could. Anyone watching would, he hoped, think he was flirting with the nurse.

"Yeah?"

"Alvarez."

She blinked at him. "Zhorchow came for him yesterday, midafternoon. Said Saunders wanted him shipped back to Earth." She winked, her serious words at odds with the flirtatious expression on her face. Griffin hoped that his own playacting was half as good as hers.

"So Zhorchow took him?" he said.

"Naw, that little phony wouldn't dirty his hands," she said with contempt. "He had a couple of UN guards with him. I stabilized the bed and they rolled him out."

Griffin thought about that for a moment. "Did he say anything? Alvarez, I mean."

"Naw, he was sleeping like a baby. He did wake up once, just after he got to sickbay. Said something to the doc, but I was busy at the med station and didn't hear what he said. And when I got back to him, he was sleeping again."

"Sleeping," Griffin echoed. "Mirren knocked him out?"

Lukas opened her mouth, then closed it again.

"I guess," she said, after a minute.

Griffin hesitated, looking at her, then took her hand in both of his and leaned forward.

"Marie. Listen. Private Michaels said he talked with Charlie Becker, the Gate tech. Becker said the Gate was only used once yesterday, to transport the bodies back to Earth."

The nurse's hand lay still for a moment, then clenched.

"Then where's Private Alvarez?" she said, and it wasn't a question. She pulled her hand away. "Go read that paper, soldier boy," she said quietly. "And then get rid of it."

She pushed back her chair and stood. "I'm beside you," she said. "Don't forget that."

Griffin nodded in thanks, and headed straight for his billet.

Chapter Forty

The Jensen Ultra, being a top-flight diagnostic machine modified to help even a doofus figure out its scan, had helpfully provided not only the scan results, but a paragraph at the bottom explaining those results.

The paragraph talked about DNA sequences and mitochondria and what they both meant.

It discussed everything it had done to try to match the genetic structure of the tiny lily.

It boasted about how it had connected to the resident AI and searched its databases, and gloried in the announcement that it had, finally, made a full and complete identification of the material.

The plant was, down to the tiniest twist of its DNA, unarguably a fine example of *Lilium pardalinum*, also known as the Leopard Lily, not a hybrid but a species.

And it had been entirely, irrevocably, and provably extinct for well over seventy-five years.

Griffin frowned at these results. The lily was real, it existed right now, in the atrium, growing away. And he had taken one of its flowers to Marie Lukas, and she had held that real flower in her hand, and fed that real flower into the Jensen Ultra. Which proved it to be extinct.

What the hell did that mean?

He was going to put the report back in his pocket when he remembered Marie Lukas telling him that that piece of paper represented her life.

He took the paper into the bathroom, turned on the tap in the sink, and let the water run over the paper. The paper slowly shredded in his palm, and he watched the fibers slide down the drain, thinking about Mirren and Zhorchow. And Private Alvarez. *Access denied.* He shook the last scraps off his hand and touched his cheek, feeling the precious dampness.

And, finally, he went to find Michaels, ready to accept what the man had been saying from the beginning. Something was wrong, desperately, seriously wrong. And if Griffin was going home to Jenny, he needed to figure this out. He needed, for her sake more than his, to keep himself safe.

He queried the door to Michaels' room, and to his surprise it didn't respond. Generally a door would tell you whether the room was vacant, or occupied, or whether its occupant just wanted to be alone—but Michaels' door didn't say anything at all. Griffin actually put his knuckles to it and rapped, a solid, old-fashioned gesture that was soundlessly absorbed into the Spectrastone. Nothing.

Frowning, he looked at the door. Something was different. What was it? The same shape, the same sign, the same picture of Michaels in the ID slot . . . The sign said, "Deleted."

Griffin stood still a minute, refusing to process it. No. Deleted? He's been *deleted*? This must be a mistake. They killed him? They . . . I don't believe this . . . they *killed* him?

He began pacing back and forth in front of the door, two steps forward, two back, stop and read the sign again. No. It didn't change. It continued to say the same thing. Deleted. Michaels had been *deleted*.

As in dead.

And he caught himself thinking, with wild fury, Jeez, just wait until I tell Michaels about *this* fuck-up—

An AP appeared before him, smooth and serious and oh so competent, and reminded him that he had an appointment with his C.O. Griffin stared at her a moment, then cursed and turned away. Saunders could wait—Griffin was going to talk to Charlie Becker.

Chapter Forty-One

They killed her," the Gate tech said raggedly. Griffin stared at him, shocked. It looked like Charlie Becker hadn't slept in days. Bloodshot eyes stared through the thick lenses.

"Killed who?" Griffin said.

"Elizabeth," Charlie replied, choking. "Oh, maybe they didn't pull the trigger, maybe they didn't poison her, or electrocute her, or drown her—"

"Charlie—"

"Or stab her, or push her out an airlock, or—"

"Charlie, snap out of it!" Griffin shouted.

"Oh!" Becker turned away, fumbled for something in his pocket, and finally produced a tattered piece of cloth. He blew his nose into it and stuffed it back in his pocket.

"But they did kill her," he said, more calmly. "They made her miserable, they really did. Whatever she did, it was because they gave her no choice. I know."

Griffin remembered Dr. Marks in the hallway, saying to Colonel Saunders, *I don't know who I am anymore.* And, *How can you know what we're doing is right?*

He put his hand on Becker's shoulder. "Charlie, I believe you," he said.

"You do?" Becker looked at him. "I barely know whether to believe myself, any more."

"I think they killed my friend Michaels," Griffin said. "I need your help, Charlie. Can you help me?"

Becker just turned away. "What good would it do? Elizabeth is dead."

Griffin felt a stab of impatience, and pushed it away.

"Charlie, I need you to tell me about yesterday," he said. "About the Gate yesterday. How many times did you—"

"One time," Becker said with weary flatness. "Just one time. To move those two bodies. Bodies don't take as much energy as living people, you know. Because you don't have to do redundancy checks so much. So it was pretty easy."

Griffin bit his lip. "Nothing else? No one living?"

"Two bodies," Becker repeated. "Dead ones. I would have known."

Griffin thought for a moment. Before him, the Gate rose silently toward the lights above. "Can anyone else run the Gate?" he asked.

"No," Charlie said, still sadly. "I talked to them about that, you know. I said to Saunders, I said what if I get sick? What if something happens to me? Who's going to run the Gate?" He rested his fingers on the control board. "He said not to worry about it. That it would be OK." Charlie looked up at Griffin. "That's another reason, you know. Why I think we're in maybe Sumatra. Or Tahiti, maybe it's Tahiti. Because maybe we don't really need the Gate at all, you see. Someone could always send a skivver. Or a ship."

"Tahiti," Griffin echoed.

"Oh, yes. Or perhaps Tobago." Charlie nodded. "I saw the outside once, you know. Before they had finished building the station. I went into a sector that wasn't finished. By mistake." He smiled. "It's really pretty out there. But I didn't tell anyone. And the workers, you know, they must have sent them home in a skivver, or a ship, or something. I brought them in through the Gate, but. . . ."

He stopped talking, as though a mainspring inside him had wound down. Griffin touched his shoulder again. Elizabeth Marks, Private Michaels, perhaps the workers who had built this station. Alonzo, Tisch—even Charlie Becker, broken on the wheel of somebody's ambitions. He thought he knew whose.

He was poised to ask another question when the main door suddenly irised open and Captain

Zhorchow strode in, followed by two UN guards. Becker yelped, wide-eyed, and scuttled backward. He put his hands up, sheltering his face, and cringed back against the Gate control panel.

Zhorchow ignored the tech. He marched to Griffin, planted his hands at his hips, and glared. Griffin put his shoulders back.

"In case you had forgotten, Private Griffin," Zhorchow said frigidly, "you have an appointment with Colonel Saunders. You are late."

"No, I'm not," Griffin replied, as coldly as the Captain. "I think that I'm probably right on time."

Zhorchow moved his head, and the guards flanked Griffin, grabbed his arms, and muscled him out of the room. Behind him, he heard Charlie Becker whimper again.

Chapter Forty-Two

I'll bet that really makes you feel big," Griffin said
furiously, and his anger felt wonderful. He
leaned against the glass side of the lift, crowd-
ed against the two guards who still held his arms.
Captain Zhorchow stared straight ahead.

Griffin snorted. "Did you enjoy threatening
Becker, or beating him, or whatever you did to that
poor little wimp? Do you love the idea that he's a
broken man?"

Zhorchow ignored him.

"Alvarez—hell, he probably wasn't a problem at
all, less than Charlie Becker. The man was drugged
out, after all. Was it even satisfying, Zhorchow? Did
you get off on eliminating a wounded man?"

Zhorchow's eyelid quivered. Gad, Griffin thought
admiringly, the man really was made of ice.

"How about my buddy Michaels," Griffin continued. "I'll bet he was more of a challenge. But you
don't have a mark on you—so my guess is that you

got him while he was sleeping. Or had your goons do it for you. That seems more your style, doesn't it, Zhorchow? That way, you don't have to mess up that perfect hair."

Without changing expression, Zhorchow hit him in the mouth. Griffin's head banged against the side of the lift, and the bright metallic taste of blood filled his mouth. The goons holding him hadn't even moved.

The captain stared at his own hand. He had cut it against Griffin's teeth, and it bled a little onto the captain's pristine uniform.

"Gotcha," Griffin whispered, and smiled.

The remnants of a meal were scattered across Saunders' desk. The colonel looked up from a small screen as Zhorchow, Griffin, and his escort walked in, then rose abruptly, his brows drawn together in anger.

"What is this?" he demanded.

"He resisted," Captain Zhorchow said offhandedly, almost as if he didn't care whether the colonel believed him or not.

"Captain, you are on report," Saunders snapped. "You will remain in your billet until I have time for you. You two, dismissed."

Zhorchow didn't move for a moment, his face

absolutely rigid, then spun about and left, trailed by the two guards. Watching them go, Griffin suddenly felt endangered, as though he had been somehow safer with the captain present. He looked at Saunders, who tossed him the napkin from his desk.

"Clean yourself up," the colonel ordered. "Zhorchow is a fool, but he doesn't explode without help. I have no sympathy for you."

"I haven't asked for any. Sir." Griffin replied.

The colonel sat and put his hands flat on the surface of his desk.

"Private Michaels has been spreading seditious sentiments," Saunders said.

"Private Michaels has been deleted," Griffin said. "Can you tell me why?"

Saunders ignored him. "Did he ever lead you to believe there might be a problem with the VR augmentation? Or that the UN is lying about the nature of our mission here?"

Griffin just looked at him.

"Have these seditions spread, Private Griffin? Did Michaels talk to anyone other than yourself?"

His hands were almost white against the surface of the desk. Griffin looked at them, and suddenly wondered why Saunders was even bothering to talk to him. He looked at Saunders' face, and read nothing there.

"I don't know. Sir."

"What were you and he doing in Central Processing last night?"

Griffin's shoulders tensed. "We were reviewing our personnel records."

There was a moment of silence.

"Thank you, Private. That's all I need to know." Saunders face was cold as ice again, all semblance of friendliness dropped. "You are dismissed."

For a moment, Griffin was tempted to let go of his temper, to challenge the colonel and demand answers to all the questions about Alvarez, and Michaels, and Marks, about AJ3905, and the Gate, and everything else. But he kept seeing the sign on Michaels' door, the word "DELETED," and kept his temper in check. If they had done it to Michaels, they could do it to Andrew Griffin. And then he would never know the truth.

Chapter Forty-Three

He slammed back into his room. The pills Michaels had given him were still lying in plain sight on the counter in his bathroom. He snatched them up and clenched his hand. The pill case cut into his palm. He opened his fist and stared at the three white pills resting on his palm. Michaels had been deleted.

He got a glass of water from the bathroom, popped the pills out of their packet, and swallowed all of them at once.

Weariness hit him with terrifying speed. As he staggered toward his bed, he feared coma or poisoning and he thought about calling for Dr. Mirren. Fear of what might happen if he called for help was more intense still.

He was dreaming even before he closed his eyes, images and sounds streaming through his consciousness in wild disorder, like the rushing of a river whose dam has cracked. Michaels was right—

Myadonna suppressed dreams and the pills were the antidote.

But was there an antidote for the dreams?

The landscape of his dreams screamed with fear and guilt. A green beast turned its inhumanly calm face toward his and said, "Three hundred cc Myadonna nitrate delivered daily." He cried out and it smiled.

Jenny's face appeared, as she once was, the clear skin and warm eyes. She said, "We killed our mother." Griffin knew she was talking about the Earth itself. He reached for her with longing and she looked into a distance which roiled with smoke. He heard the sirens, and tried to warn her not to go, not to drive that car.

Dr. Marks stood beside her, smiling into his eyes, her face alight with a frightening joy. "I want to create!" she said and Jenny's lips moved in the same words. "I want that!" She opened her hands in a gesture of longing and acceptance. "I want to have a baby!" she said, and Jenny was speaking the same words but he could not hear her voice.

Dr. Marks *had* created. She had created the Quantum Gate and it had brought them all here.

Michaels was behind him, saying "Dr. Marks took a walk!" Saunders was everywhere, and his voice said, "All operations are being governed. . . "

Jenny opened her mouth again, and a flying bug emerged from her mouth, spread its wings in

joyous beauty, then shattered as his laser seared
through it.

Chapter Forty-Four

An alarm blasted through Griffin's unquiet sleep, making his heart race and confusing his still-dreaming mind. He opened his eyes. The air roared with the incessant beeping.

"What the hell is going on? What is that—?"

The AP's voice rang through the air. "Level One alert. All combat troops to the egress chamber."

Griffin rolled from his bunk, amazed at how the training took over. He was dressing even before he was fully awake.

"Level One alert. Level One alert."

The door opened in front of him as he almost ran into the entry way, still closing his shirt. And there he froze, staring at Michaels' door. It still said DELETED.

"Level One alert," said the relentless voice of the AP, "All able-bodied troops to the egress chamber."

Michaels and Alvarez.

His feet took him down the short entrance way

and out into the hall.

"Full-scale assault in progress. All combat troops to the egress chamber."

Dr. Marks, and Charlie Becker.

The lift opened, humming, and he ran into Sergeant Cranshaw. Before he could even formulate the thought, he had grabbed her by the shoulder and dragged her into a niche. She turned, arms already raised for the chop, before she saw his face and froze.

"Michaels," Griffin said. "What happened to Michaels?"

Her eyes narrowed. "Private Michaels' contract was revoked."

"Revoked! Was Private Michaels killed?" Griffin asked. "For god's sake, Sergeant! What did they do to him?"

She didn't reply, and Griffin stared in growing horror at her face.

"You got rid of him, didn't you?" he whispered. "You did it for them."

"I'm a professional soldier," Maria Cranshaw said flatly. "My superiors give me orders, and I follow them. It's my job."

"How could you? He was your lover—my god, Sergeant! What did they promise you?"

For a moment, it looked as if he might have gotten through to her. "He asked me that, too," the sergeant said, and then the military mask clamped down again. "It's a raid, soldier," she said, her voice clipped. "If it were up to me, you'd be confined to quarters. But in case you haven't noticed, we're a little understaffed right now."

They stared at each other for a moment, and the air between them seemed to crackle with tension.

"Go suit up," she finally ordered. "You're a soldier, Griffin. A fighter. It's your job.".

She pushed him away. Griffin rushed down the hall toward the airlock, pursued by questions.

An extinct lily, a million ugly lies, and some even uglier truths.

The airlock emergency lights flashed red, and the suits hanging on the walls looked like medieval armor in rows. The door's sign said DANGER. He felt like giggling for a crazy heartbeat, then hooked down a suit. Beside him, Castle and Hawkins and Cranshaw struggled into their own suits, and Hynick babbled, a cascade of words that nobody listened to except perhaps for Whalen, who broke her grieving silence.

"Shut up, Hynick," she said, and her voice sounded rusty and used up. "Just shut up."

Hynick didn't stop. Perhaps he couldn't.

"Chamber ready for decompression," said the AP. "Please don VR helmet and activate envirosuit."

Griffin stepped into the suit and clumsily flattened the seams around him. The seams wriggled like snakes on his body as the suit corrected the fit.

He pulled the helmet over his head, and the sound of Hynick's voice cut off abruptly.

Where were the workers who built the station? What had they done with Alvarez? What had they promised Maria Cranshaw, to get her to eliminate her lover? And what, he wondered suddenly, would they promise whoever was chosen to kill him?

The TopHat flickered, then flared into brilliant life. He faced the airlock door, waiting for the cycle to complete.

Remove the helmet outside and the self-destruct is activated. Don't you know what that atmosphere does to a man? But the skivvers weren't corroded.

The dangerous door opened, and he was outside.

Outside, standing on AJ3905's surface. The swirling sky filled his field of vision. Brown sere land, rolling hills. All of it familiar from the sim runs, but something seemed missing.

The helmet told him Captain Hiaumet was in command. His voice came clear in Griffin's ears. "Look, everybody stay on your toes. Right? There are bugs *everywhere*."

And that was it, he realized. The bloodlust, the eagerness—it was entirely gone, leaving him standing in the monochrome landscape with no compulsion to kill.

He turned slowly. Hawkins and Whalen were facing away from him, but Sergeant Cranshaw's helmet faced him straight on.

His suit's alarm spoke. "Alien presence, no lock available. Danger." A red arrow appeared on his display, pointing left. He turned quickly but saw nothing. "Alien proximity alert. No lock available." Where? Where was it?

"Warning. Foe behind. Danger. Please look down. Warning."

"I've got him, I've got him," Maria Cranshaw's voice shouted, and Griffin watched in horror as she raised her rifle and pointed it directly at him.

"Sarge! No!" He yelled. She didn't even slow down. Griffin flung himself sideways, the clumsy suit ruining his balance. He rolled swiftly away. She pursued him, her rifle raised again. He raised his own rifle.

"Sarge! Stop!"

She took aim, and he sent a beam of red light shooting past her. She leaped to one side.

"Almost got me," her voice reported calmly. "Looks like one of the ground huggers, but the armament is new."

Ground huggers? What did she mean?

The VR, he realized. He had taken the antidote, so the drug didn't work in him anymore. But it did in Sergeant Cranshaw, and the other members of Phoenix Company.

And the drug and VR, together, were telling them that Andrew Griffin was a bug.

And if they would lie about that—they would

lie about AJ3905. About chlorine that didn't corrode skivvers. About a green paradise so beautiful it leaked through their perverted VR equipment. Even if it wasn't entirely a lie, Griffin thought, it was more than enough evidence for him. He didn't believe them—and it was time to do something about it.

He started to reach for his helmet, but Hawkins had found him now. The big man crept around an outcropping of rock, weapon raised and ready.

"Ah, Jeez, Hawk," Griffin shouted, and rolled quickly away behind a bush. His weapon banged awkwardly against his legs, but he couldn't take the time to stop it. He tore at the fasteners on the helmet.

The display's darkness broke into a readout. "Life Support error: #120.AB. Suit environment breached," it said.

He tore more furiously at the helmet. Hawkins and Cranshaw had lost him, but it was only a matter of time—

"Prior to euthanization—" said his suit.

Oh, no! The SD device.

The display screen changed, "VR damaged, suit breached, two injuries."

The suit's relentless voice continued, "Your employment contract entitles you to make peace with the universe and or God, as you perceive he, she, or it. Euthanasia will occur in fifteen seconds."

No! As he flipped the fasteners opened, Cranshaw rose suddenly from the far side of the bush, scanning the area, her weapon ready. He carefully lifted his rifle and centered the targeting image on her. His finger slid onto the trigger as he watched his sergeant search for him. A shining red ball appeared in his helmet display. The numerals "15" wrapped across its surface. Cranshaw seemed to move in slow motion, scanning the area, closer and closer to the slight depression in which he lay. The numbers changed.

Tisch. Alonzo. Alvarez. Marks.

Michaels.

The display in his helmet briefly scattered into static colors, then the ball changed. Thirteen.

Cranshaw stopped turning—she had spotted him. The muzzle of the rifle swung toward him with dreadful and inexorable slowness.

Twelve.

Griffin didn't even hesitate. He killed her.

Eleven.

He threw the rifle aside and groped for the helmet clasps. A woman's face flashed into his field of vision like a dream, and then vanished. Ten.

The suit's voice changed. "Warning. Helmet seal is broken."

He tried to pull the helmet off. It stuck. He yanked at the connections again. Suddenly, the helmet was coming off.

The helmet's edge cleared his eyes. He looked into the face of a lovely but strangely dressed woman who had soft, curly blond hair. She was framed by a bright blue sky with clouds—a sky so clear it looked scrubbed, fresh, and clean. The woman's lips moved, but he couldn't hear her words. The air on his face was soft and aromatic with growing things. A bird sang.

"Oh, my God! Michaels was right. They're *human*."

Lies. All lies. The sane ones lied and the crazy man told the truth. He had believed the mind and not the heart.

Not bugs, but *human*. How could that be? A voice in his head replayed a part of the orientation lecture, a part he'd heard but had not understood—a Quantum Gate reached into the parallel reality frequencies surrounding our own. Oh, God, no. Becker and DiSilva were both right. The Gate didn't really transport to a different place, and yet this also wasn't really the same place either. This was Earth but it was a different Earth, one not destroyed or not destroyed yet.

The woman tugged at his suit. He undid the seals and rolled free of it, flinching as something pinched at his side and grew cold. Nearby, Cranshaw's motionless envirosuit lay sprawled across the emerald grass.

Griffin looked away from it and saw a helmeted CO suit approaching. From his helmet nearby he heard Hawkins' voice say, "Cranshaw down, got a bug on her. Trying to get clear shot."

He couldn't kill Hawkins. He wouldn't. He looked around desperately, and a heavy object hit him from behind as the rifle flashed.

He went down. He was still alive. Would he remain that way? He didn't know. He did know that he wasn't in hiding anymore. As he closed his eyes against the stunning blue of the sky, he smiled.

Hardback

In The 1st Degree: A Novel $19.95
Dominic Stone

The 7th Guest: A Novel $21.95
Matthew J. Costello and Craig Shaw Gardner

Paperback

Hell: A Cyberpunk Thriller—A Novel $5.99
Chet Williamson

Masterminds of Falkenstein: A Castle Falkenstein Novel $5.99
John DeChancie

The Pandora Directive: A Tex Murphy Novel $5.99
Aaron Conners

From Prussia with Love: A Castle Falkenstein Novel $5.99
John DeChancie

Realms of Arkania: The Charlatan—A Novel $5.99
Ulrich Kiesow
Translated by Amy Katherine Kile

Realms of Arkania: The Lioness—A Novel $5.99
Ina Kramer
Translated by Amy Katherine Kile

Roger Zelazny and Jane Lindskold's Chronomaster—A Novel $5.99
Jane Lindskold

Star Control: Interbellum—A Novel $5.99
W.T. Quick

Star Crusader: A Novel $5.99
Bruce Balfour

Wizardry: The League of the Crimson Crescent—A Novel $5.99
James Reagan

X-COM UFO Defense: A Novel $5.99
Diane Duane

FILL IN AND MAIL TODAY

PRIMA PUBLISHING
P.O. Box 1260BK
Rocklin, CA 95677

USE YOUR VISA/MC AND ORDER BY PHONE
(916) 632-4400 (M-F 9:00-4:00 PST)

Please send me the following titles:

Quantity	Title	Amount
_____	_____	_____
_____	_____	_____
_____	_____	_____
_____	_____	_____
	Subtotal	$_____
	Postage & Handling	
	($4.00 for the first book plus	
	$1.00 each additional book)	$ _____
	Sales Tax	
	7.25% California only	
	8.25% Tennessee only	
	5.00% Maryland only	
	7.00% General Service Tax Canada	$_____
	TOTAL (U.S. funds only)	$_____

❑ Check enclosed for $_____(payable to Prima Publishing)
Charge my ❑ Master Card ❑ Visa

Account No._____ Exp. Date _____

Signature _____

Your Name_____

Address _____

City/State/Zip _____

Daytime Telephone_____

Satisfaction is guaranteed—or your money back!
Please allow three to four weeks for delivery.

THANK YOU FOR YOUR ORDER

JANE E. HAWKINS is a mathematician and computer programmer. She lives in Seattle, Washington.